STEP IN THE DARK

FRANCIS DURBRIDGE

WILLIAMS & WHITING

Cover design by
Timo Schroeder

9781912582624

Williams & Whiting (Publishers)

15 Chestnut Grove, Hurstpierpoint,

West Sussex, BN6 9SS

Titles by Francis Durbridge published by Williams & Whiting

Murder At The Weekend – the rediscovered newspaper serials and short stories

Also published by Williams & Whiting:
Francis Durbridge : The Complete Guide
By Melvyn Barnes

Titles by Francis Durbridge to be published by Williams & Whiting

A Case For Paul Temple
A Game of Murder
A Man Called Harry Brent
A Time of Day
Bat Out of Hell
Breakaway – A Family Affair
Breakaway – The Local Affair
Melissa
Murder In The Media
My Friend Charles
One Man To Another – a novel
Paul Temple and the Alex Affair
Paul Temple and the Canterbury Case (film script)
Paul Temple and the Conrad Case
Paul Temple and the Geneva Mystery
Paul Temple and the Gilbert Case
Paul Temple and the Gregory Affair
Paul Temple and the Jonathan Mystery
Paul Temple and the Lawrence Affair
Paul Temple and the Madison Mystery
Paul Temple and the Margo Mystery
Paul Temple and the Sullivan Mystery
Paul Temple and the Vandyke Affair
Paul Temple Intervenes
The Desperate People
The Doll
The World of Tim Frazer
Tim Frazer and the Salinger Affair
Tim Frazer and the Mellin Forrest Mystery
Two Paul Temple Plays for Television

INTRODUCTION

Francis Durbridge (1912-98) was a prolific writer of sketches, stories and plays for BBC radio from 1933. At first they were mostly light entertainments, including libretti for musical comedies, but in 1938 he created novelist/detective Paul Temple and his wife Steve in the radio serial *Send for Paul Temple* – attracting over 7,000 fan letters and ensuring that the Temples were permanently launched. This resulted in twenty more Temple cases, from *Paul Temple and the Front Page Men* (1938) to *Paul Temple and the Geneva Mystery* (1965), plus new productions of some of the serials. In addition the Temples acquired an impressive European following, with translations broadcast in the Netherlands from 1939, Germany from 1949, Italy from 1953 and Denmark from 1954.

Then from 1952, while continuing with the Temples on the radio, Durbridge turned to television and rapidly became known for teasing viewers with red herrings, cliff-hanger endings to each episode, and the certainty that no character should be believed whatever they might say. And as with his radio serials he conquered Europe, with numerous television productions in at least six countries until the 1980s.

In comparison Durbridge's contributions to the cinema were more limited in number, beginning with four Paul Temple films adapted from his early radio serials. *Send for Paul Temple* (Butchers/Nettlefold, 1946) was based on his 1938 radio serial of the same name, with a screenplay by John Argyle and Durbridge, produced/directed by Argyle and starring Anthony Hulme and Joy Shelton. This was followed by *Calling Paul Temple* (Butchers/Nettlefold, 1948), based on his 1945 radio serial *Send for Paul Temple Again*, with a screenplay by Durbridge, A.R. Rawlinson and Kathleen Butler, produced by Ernest G. Roy and directed by Maclean Rogers, starring John Bentley and Dinah Sheridan. Thirdly there was *Paul Temple's*

Triumph (Butchers/Nettlefold, 1950), based on his 1939 radio serial *News of Paul Temple*, with a screenplay by A.R. Rawlinson, produced by Ernest G. Roy and directed by Maclean Rogers, and again starring John Bentley and Dinah Sheridan. And finally, *Paul Temple Returns* (Butchers/Nettlefold, 1952) was based on his 1942 radio serial *Paul Temple Intervenes*, with a screenplay by Durbridge, produced by Ernest G. Roy and directed by Maclean Rogers, but this time pairing John Bentley with Patricia Dainton.

Hot on the heels of those four Paul Temple films came cinema adaptations of Durbridge's first five television serials. *The Broken Horseshoe* (Butchers/Nettlefold, 1953) was based on his 1952 television serial of the same name, with a screenplay by A.R. Rawlinson, produced by Ernest G. Roy and directed by Martyn C. Webster. Then came *Operation Diplomat* (Butchers/Nettlefold, 1953), based on his 1952 television serial of the same name, with a screenplay by A.R. Rawlinson and John Guillermin, produced by Ernest G. Roy and directed by Guillermin. Next was *The Teckman Mystery* (Corona/British Lion, 1954), based on his 1953/54 television serial *The Teckman Biography*, with a screenplay by Durbridge and James Matthews, produced by Josef Somlo and directed by Wendy Toye. Then followed *Portrait of Alison* (Insignia/Anglo Amalgamated, 1955), based on his 1955 television serial of the same name, with a screenplay by Ken Hughes and Guy Green, produced by Frank Godwin and directed by Guy Green. And finally there was *The Vicious Circle* (Romulus/Beaconsfield/Independent Film Distributors, 1957), based on his 1956 television serial *My Friend Charles*, with a screenplay by Durbridge, produced by Peter Rogers and directed by Gerald Thomas.

Although Durbridge did not completely abandon writing for the cinema, he must have been hampered by the fact that films had moved into the crash-bang-wallop and sock-in-the-jaw mode that contrasted sharply with his sophisticated and very British style. But recent discoveries in his archives have revealed that he wrote the screenplay *Step in the Dark* and a film synopsis called *Tim Frazer and the Melvin Affair*, and he also wrote something potentially sensational after the acclaimed film producer Dino De Laurentiis commissioned him to write a major movie. So in 1962 Durbridge produced a treatment of over one hundred pages for *Zakary*, an enthralling story of espionage and personal relationships with a Japanese setting spanning the years from 1910 to just after the 1941 attack on Pearl Harbor. This had the makings of a cinema blockbuster – but very sadly, as with countless projects by screenwriters over the years, it never saw the light of day.

Turning specifically to his screenplay *Step in the Dark*, this was not produced as a cinema film in the UK but it now appears that it was translated and produced in Germany. The rather unfortunate result was *Piccadilly null Uhr zwölf* (Piccadilly Zero Hour Twelve), Divina-Film 1963, with a screenplay by Rudolf Zehetgruber, produced by Ilse Kubaschewski and Eberhard Meichsner and directed by Zehetgruber. Although this film bears no comparison whatsoever with Durbridge's screenplay (except for the names of several characters), his name appeared on the film credits and posters and was doubtless a promotional ploy that took advantage of his enormous popularity in Germany.

So it was early in the 1960s that Francis Durbridge wrote his ill-fated screenplay *Step in the Dark*, but now we can be comforted by the fact that it later resurfaced in a different and more acceptable guise. The novel *The Pig-Tail Murder* was published in May 1969 by Hodder & Stoughton, and although it has hitherto been regarded as a one-off original novel it can now be seen to follow *Step in the Dark* very closely. As always, the book enjoyed success in European translations – in Germany as *Im Schatten von Soho*, in France as *L'Enfant au cerf-volant*, in Italy as *Mezz'ora per vivere, mezz'ora per morire*, in the Netherlands as *De haarvlecht*, in Poland as *Warkocz śmierci* and in Slovenia as *Papirnati zmaj*.

More happily therefore, after the travesty of the German film, we can finally welcome Durbridge's original screenplay in print to stand beside the faithful novelisation.

Melvyn Barnes
Author of *Francis Durbridge: The Complete Guide* (Williams & Whiting, 2018)

STEP IN THE DARK

An original screenplay
by

FRANCIS DURBRIDGE

WILLIAMS AND WHITING

PRINCIPAL CHARACTERS:

Della Morris
Detective Sergeant Jack Bellamy
Chief Superintendent O'Day
Ingrid
Mike Hilton
Selby Brooks
Ruth Hilton
Detective Inspector Craddock
Nigel Green
Peter Lloyd
Louis Dubinsky
Ruby Stevenson
Chris Benson
Iris
Vida
Bob West
Mrs Cliff
Boy
Desk Sergeant
Police Doctor
Sergeant
Policeman
Alice Thorpe
Sergeant Roberts
Barmaid
Peg
Girl in bookshop
Myrtle
Mrs Poole
Girl with ball

OPEN TO: A Soho Street. London. Night.
Sleepy, blues-type music is heard as we move slowly down the street.

THE TITLES AND CREDITS COME UP ON THE SCREEN.

It is about ten o'clock and the bars and restaurants are crowded, but the street is practically empty. Neon signs of restaurants and coffee bars are seen. Italian, French, Greek, Hungarian. We stop at the neon sign which reads: PARIS PLAISIR – Non-Stop Revue. The music changes abruptly to an ear-piercing trumpet solo.

FADE OUT TITLES.

CUT TO: Paris Plaisir. Soho. Night.
In the auditorium, a sea of hypnotised, droop-mouthed faces. On stage, a human sacrifice. Bust-bouncing savages, wielding spears, dance around a writhing brunette named DELLA. As the trumpet reaches its crescendo the GIRLS plunge their spears into the body of DELLA. The curtains close. There is wild applause. The GIRLS chatter as they move to the wings.

CUT TO: DELLA's Dressing Room at Paris Plaisir. Night.
DELLA enters, going quickly to the dressing table. Suddenly she freezes. There is a man's trilby hat on the dressing table. She turns to see JACK BELLAMY, his feet resting on the wash basin as he lounges in the chair. A rugged thirty-year old, with penetrating eyes, there is something ominous in the way JACK BELLAMY smiles.
DELLA: What are you doing here?
BELLAMY rises and moves down to DELLA.
BELLAMY: I thought we might continue our little chat, Della.

3

DELLA: (*Tensely*) I can't talk now. I've got to change.
            I've only got three minutes.
BELLAMY: It won't take you a minute to tell me what I
            want to know.
DELLA: (*Agitated*) Look – I've told you everything!
            There's nothing else to tell … Now, will you
            please leave me alone!

*As DELLA turns towards the wardrobe, BELLAMY takes hold
of her arm; he stands holding her for a moment.*

BELLAMY: Della, it's no use! You've got to tell me! I've
            got to know who he is …
DELLA: (*Trying to free herself*) I've told you – I don't
            know who he is! I don't know anything about
            him!
BELLAMY: I don't believe you!

*DELLA looks at BELLAMY; worried and hesitant. There is the
sudden sound of voices in the corridor outside. The door is
partly opened by one of the CHORUS GIRLS. The GIRL stands
in the corridor talking to someone.*

DELLA: (*Worried; glancing towards the door*) I'll see
            you   later. I'll come to the flat, we can talk
            there …
BELLAMY: You said that last time, and you didn't show up.
DELLA: Yes, I know, but – I'll come tonight … I
            promise …

BELLAMY hesitates, then slowly releases DELLA's arm.

BELLAMY: All right. Pick up a cab as soon as you finish
            here. I'll be waiting for you.

*BELLAMY takes his hat from the dressing table and crosses to
the door.*

CUT TO: The Soho Street. Night.
*JACK BELLAMY comes down the steps of the entrance to the
Paris Plaisir and walks along the street, taking out a packet of*

4

cigarettes as he does so. He stops to light a cigarette. A police car glides into shot. BELLAMY flicks away the spent match as the car door opens. He steps into the car and it moves away.

CUT TO: Inside the Police Car. Night.
There is a uniformed DRIVER. In the rear seat, next to BELLAMY, is CHIEF SUPERINTENDENT O'DAY who is tough, cynical, but not completely unlikeable. JACK BELLAMY's manner is no longer ominous; simply serious and business-like.

O'DAY: Good evening, Sergeant. Did you exercise your undoubted charm on the young lady?
BELLAMY: Yes, but I didn't get very far. I'm seeing her again.
O'DAY: When?
BELLAMY: Tonight.
O'DAY: Where?
BELLAMY: At my place. (*He notices O'DAY's expression*) Don't worry, she'll turn up this time.
O'DAY: And you think she'll talk?
BELLAMY: Yes, I do, sir.
O'DAY: Well, I hope you're right because none of the other girls will. They're scared to death of the little bastard.

CUT TO: A street in Notting Hill Gate. London. Night.
A quiet street of three-storeyed houses.
The police car stops near a mews and JACK BELLAMY gets out. He waves and the car pulls away. He walks quickly into the nearby mews.

CUT TO: JACK BELLAMY's Flat. Notting Hill Gate. Night.
Three hours later.

JACK BELLAMY is in a dressing gown at a small table, mixing drinks. The radio is playing nearby. He hears something and switches off the radio. He peers through the curtains, glancing down into the mews. He looks thoughtful for a moment, then moves to the door.

CUT TO: The Landing of BELLAMY's Flat. Night.
BELLAMY comes out of his flat and moves to the top of the stairs.

CUT TO: The Main Hall and Stairs. Night.
BELLAMY stands at the top of the stairs and looks down. DELLA stands in the open street-doorway. She stares up at BELLAMY and with a strange, confused expression.
BELLAMY: I didn't know it was open. Come on up!
BELLAMY turns to move back to his flat, then hesitates, looking back at DELLA who is still standing there, gazing up at him. Suddenly, she lurches forward – clutching the stair banister for support.
BELLAMY: Della!
BELLAMY runs down to DELLA who topples over, her face still staring up at him. BELLAMY temporarily freezes as he looks down at the girl's staring face. He kneels, slowly reaching out to her. As he turns her over, we hear once again the harsh music – the blaring trumpet as in DELLA's stage performance. For the first time we see the knife in DELLA's back.

CUT TO: The El Sombrero Coffee Bar. Chelsea. Afternoon.
There are sombrero-shaped ashtrays. Spanish looks waiters – everything has a Spanish flavour but the food.
INGRID sits in an alcove waiting for JACK BELLAMY. She is a professional call-girl in her early twenties; a good looking blonde from Stockholm. INGRID's manner is tense; nervous.

6

Her sombrero is full of cigarette ends. She is glancing at her watch as BELLAMY arrives and slips into the chair opposite her.

INGRID: You're late.

BELLAMY: Yes, I know.

INGRID: You said half past one.

BELLAMY: (*Taking out cigarettes*) That's right.

INGRID: I've got to leave soon, they're expecting me back at the shop.

BELLAMY: They'll wait.

A pause.

INGRID: (*Hesitant*) It's a long time, Jack.

BELLAMY: Yes, long time no see.

INGRID: (*Nervously*) Why – why did you send for me?

BELLAMY: (*Lighting a cigarette*) You've heard about Della?

INGRID: Della?

BELLAMY: Della Morris. She was murdered. It was in the papers.

INGRID: (*Obviously lying*) I – I don't know anyone called Della. I never read the papers these days, they're too depressing.

BELLAMY watches INGRID.

BELLAMY: (*A touch of sarcasm*) My mistake, I thought she was a friend of yours.

INGRID: No – No, she wasn't …

BELLAMY slowly replaces his lighter and smiles at INGRID.

BELLAMY: Ingrid, I reckon I've been pretty nice to you, one way and another …

INGRID: Yes. Yes, you have …

BELLAMY: I fixed that labour permit, remember?

INGRID: Of course I remember. I was very grateful.

BELLAMY: Was? (*Still smiling at INGRID*) I hope you still are, Sweetie.

7

INGRID:	Yes, I'm still grateful.
BELLAMY:	(*The smile fading; a touch of anger*) Then stop pulling the wool over my eyes!
INGRID:	What do you mean?
BELLAMY:	That job of yours is a front; it always has been. I know what you're up to, Sweetie. You're back on the old beat.
INGRID:	(*Protesting*) No, Jack …
BELLAMY:	Oh, yes you are! Only this time it isn't a beat, it's a phone number, and you're working for someone. You – and the rest of the girls.
INGRID:	I don't know what you're talking about!
BELLAMY:	You know what I'm talking about, all right! (*Leaning across the table*) I'm talking about the murderous little bastard that's running this call-girl outfit. (*Gently; taking hold of INGRID's wrist*) Ingrid, you've got to tell me who he is …
INGRID:	I don't know who he is! I don't know … (*Frightened; shaking her head*) Honestly, Jack, I don't know …

BELLAMY stares at INGRID for a moment, undecided whether to believe her or not, then he slowly releases her hand.

BELLAMY: All right, Sweetie. You don't know …

CUT TO: King's Road. Chelsea. Day.
A sunny afternoon.

We see Chelsea from MIKE HILTON's eyeline as he drives his brand-new blue sports car down the King's Road. The arty, intellectual squatters of Chelsea have discarded their winter uniforms bought from the Army Surplus Stores and are emerging like butterflies in multi-coloured clothing. One of the regiment is SELBY BROOKS. We see her in the distance as MIKE's car approaches a zebra crossing. SELBY is twenty, feline-looking, in ballet-type trousers and a loose shirt, she

8

could stop traffic in any other district; here, there is merely the turning of heads. (Women would contest that the attraction is the kitten she fondles as she walks down the road, seemingly oblivious to anything else.) She stops at the zebra crossing. MIKE HILTON's car drives past – he looks annoyed and irritated. SELBY crosses the zebra and goes into The Fourposter, a public house on the other side of the road.

CUT TO: The Exterior of Tall Trees – a country house. Surrey. Day.
Tall Trees is an attractive detached house on the outskirts of Belford-on-Thames, Surrey.
The blue sports car stops on the tree-bordered drive and MIKE gets out. He still looks tired and irritated. He takes his golf clubs from the boot of the car and goes to the front door of the house, taking out his door key. He unlocks the door and enters.

CUT TO: Tall Trees. The Hall. Day.
Mike puts his golf bag in the hall stand and calls to his wife.
MIKE: Ruth!
There is no reply and he goes to the foot of the stairs.
MIKE: Ruth!
Mike looks faintly surprised, sighs irritatedly, and goes into the kitchen.

CUT TO: Tall Trees. The Kitchen. Day.
This is a luxurious, modernised kitchen with every conceivable labour-saving device.
MIKE looks around the door and seeing his wife is not there goes out.

CUT TO: Tall Trees. The Drawing Room. Day.
This is a tastefully furnished room with many antiques; but most of the paintings are modern.

MIKE enters.

MIKE: Ruth!

MIKE sighs again and is moving to the door when he notices an envelope on the mantel-shelf. He crosses the room, takes the envelope from the mantel-shelf, opens it, and reads the letter inside. He is surprised and angry. Suddenly, he makes a decision and moves quickly to the door, putting the letter in his pocket as he goes.

CUT TO: Belford-on-Thames Railway Station. Day.
MIKE's car brakes to a standstill outside the main entrance. MIKE jumps out and goes quickly into the station.

CUT TO: Belford-on-Thames   Railway   Station.   Main Platform. Day.
Several PASSENGERS are waiting for the London train. MIKE appears; he looks anxiously up and down the platform. He cannot see his wife. He sighs, starts to go, then notices the waiting room.

CUT TO: Belford-on-Thames Railway Station. The Waiting Room. Day.
A poorly dressed OLD MAN with a bag of shopping sits near the door. On the seat opposite, a suitcase on the floor beside her, sits RUTH HILTON. She is staring at one of those pictures for "Sunny Holidays", but her thoughts are obviously elsewhere.

MIKE appears in the doorway. She is not sure of him for a moment. He crosses to her. They look at one another in silence for a moment. MIKE glances at the OLD MAN, then sits beside RUTH.

RUTH: I thought you were playing golf …

MIKE: Brian didn't turn up. Look, Ruth …

RUTH: (*Tensely*) No, Mike – please! That's why I left
          while you weren't there – to avoid all this.
MIKE: (*Angrily*) Did you think I wouldn't try to find you,
          then? Did you think I'd just read your note and
          leave it at that?
RUTH: I thought you might try to be sensible – yes.
MIKE: You call this being sensible?
RUTH turns away from MIKE; she is obviously distressed.
RUTH: Mike, I don't want another row … Not here,
          please …
*MIKE hesitates; glances across awkwardly at the OLD MAN,
who is watching them with great interest. The OLD MAN looks
quickly away, and MIKE continues, much quieter.*
MIKE: I'm sorry about last night. It was my fault. I
          realise that now. I lost my temper.
RUTH: It's not just last night …
MIKE: Well, what is it? We've always made up before.
RUTH: (*Shaking her head*) During the past year we've
          had one row after another, and I just can't stand it
          any longer!
MIKE: Now, look, be reasonable! Is it my fault we
          always seem to be quarrelling?
RUTH: (*Interrupting MIKE*) I don't know whose fault it is,
          and I don't care! I only know I just can't go on
          like this …
There is a pause.
*MIKE is about to say something then, obviously unable to cope
with the situation, he changes his mind.*
MIKE: All right, if that's the way you want it.
RUTH: It isn't the way I want it, Mike – but there's no
          alternative.
MIKE: (*Suddenly exasperated*) Ruth, what's happened to
          us? What the hell's happened?

11

RUTH: (*A note of despair*) I don't know. Ever since Jill died it seems as if we …

MIKE: Oh, for God's sake don't bring Jill into this! It's over a year since we lost Jill … She hasn't anything to do with this …

RUTH: (*Quietly; looking at MIKE*) Do you believe that? Do you honestly believe that?

MIKE doesn't reply. RUTH is still looking at him.

MIKE: You think I've changed since Jill died, don't you, Ruth?

RUTH: (*Gently*) I think perhaps we've both changed, Mike. (*Turning away from MIKE*) Now leave me alone … Please leave me alone.

There is a pause.

MIKE glances across at the OLD MAN, then looks at RUTH again.

MIKE: What are you going to do?

RUTH: I'm going to stay with the Harrisons for a little while.

MIKE: And then what?

RUTH: I've been thinking about going back to my old job in Paris. If they still want me, that is.

MIKE: Been thinking? You've been planning this for some time, then?

RUTH: (*Wearily*) No, Mike, I haven't. But I don't do things on impulse, you should know that by now.

MIKE: (*Bitterly*) Yes, I suppose I should.

The train is heard coming into the station. MIKE reaches for RUTH's suitcase. There is a pair of gloves on top of it. RUTH picks it up herself. She obviously doesn't not want a scene on the platform.

RUTH: Goodbye, Mike …

MIKE refuses to speak. RUTH waits for a second, then goes out. There is the sound of voices on the platform, and the slamming of doors. Silence. Then the train pulls out.

As the sound of it dies away, MIKE turns to go. Something at his feet arrests his attention. He picks it up. It is one of RUTH's gloves. His rigid, dispassionate expression softens. He stands looking out at the platform, holding the glove.

CUT TO: The Exterior of NIGEL GREEN's Garage, Belford-on-Thames.

This is a very modern and beautifully laid-out garage on the outskirts of Belford-on-Thames. Owned by NIGEL GREEN, an ex-racing driver, the garage consists of a large double-fronted showroom with an up-to-date service station and petrol pumps. NIGEL GREEN is a main distributor for several well-known British and Continental cars; there are several superb examples in the showroom at the present moment.

DETECTIVE INSPECTOR CRADDOCK is being served with petrol as MIKE drives up to the pumps. CRADDOCK is a quiet, likeable man in his late fifties, who takes an active interest in local affairs. He gives a friendly nod as MIKE climbs out of his car.

CRADDOCK: Good morning, Mr Hilton!

MIKE: Hello, Inspector …

CRADDOCK: We've got the Orphanage party next week, sir. Can we count on you again this year?

MIKE: (*Off-hand*) Oh, I don't know. They've seen that old trick of mine too many times, Inspector. (*Relenting*) But put me down for a fiver, it'll buy the ice lollies.

CRADDOCK: (*Laughing*) Thank you, Mr Hilton.

MIKE: (*To the ATTENDANT*) Fill her up, Arthur.

MIKE nods to the smiling INSPECTOR and crosses towards the showroom.

13

CUT TO: The Car Showroom. Day.

NIGEL GREEN and PETER LLOYD are standing outside the showroom discussing the merits and otherwise of a second-hand Austin Healey. NIGEL is in his early forties; slim, well-dressed, very sure of himself. PETER LLOYD is a second-hand car salesman; a biggish man – with a slightly raffish manner. NIGEL turns as MIKE approaches.

NIGEL: (*Pleasantly*) Good morning, Mike! How's the car going?

MIKE: … I'm having a spot of bother, Nigel! She's stalling rather badly.

NIGEL: Oh, I'm sorry about that. But don't worry, we'll put it right. Drop it in on Thursday morning …

LLOYD smiles at MIKE, then looks admiringly across at the sports car.

MIKE: (*To NIGEL*) What time does this dinner start tomorrow night?

NIGEL: Half past eight. But let's have a drink first. I'll meet you in the bar.

MIKE: Yes, all right. About eight o'clock?

NIGEL: Splendid.

MIKE: See you then …

MIKE gives a friendly nod to LLOYD and strolls back to his car.

LLOYD: (*Indicating the sports car*) How much did that cost him?

NIGEL: Four and a half …

LLOYD gives a little whistle; obviously impressed.

NIGEL: Don't worry, he can afford it.

LLOYD: Who is he?

NIGEL: His name's Hilton; he's an estate agent. His old man left him half a million, apart from a whacking good business.

LLOYD: Some blighters get all the luck!

14

NIGEL: Oh, I don't know about that. His wife's just walked out on him. Nice girl, too. (*He nods towards the Austin Healey*) Well – what do you think this jalopy's worth?

LLOYD: (*Grinning*) About half what you're asking for it, old boy.

CUT TO: King's Road. Chelsea. Evening.
MIKE, dressed in a dinner jacket and wearing a white scarf, is driving his car towards the West End. The engine is spluttering badly, and he looks both fed-up and irritated. It is obvious that the car is about to stall.

CUT TO: King's Road. Chelsea. Night.
This is the same section of the King's Road and the same side of the road as seen earlier in the script.
The car has finally stalled and MIKE, head under the bonnet, is attempting to bring the car back to life, but his efforts are in vain. He closes the bonnet of the car and looks up and down the road as he feels in his pocket for some change. There is no telephone box in sight. He suddenly notices the public house on the other side of the road. He crosses towards The Fourposter.

CUT TO: The Fourposter. The Saloon Bar.
The place is jam-packed with a veritable rainbow of humanity, from the queer to the quaint, the vicious to the virtuous (though there is some considerable doubt about the last named).
There is a sudden roar of laughter from a corner of the room where there is a circle of faces. The important members of this little group are LOUIS DUBINSKY, a dumpy, friendly little man with rimless glasses, (he is Polish and owns a second-hand bookshop on the King's Road); RUBY STEVENSON, a middle-aged, flashily dressed, retired music-hall artist; CHRIS BENSON, a handsome, duffle-coated artist in his twenties; and

15

three call-girls, IRIS, VIDA and INGRID. IRIS and VIDA are brunettes and Cockney. INGRID we have already met. She is the good-looking blonde from Sweden.

SELBY BROOKS is also in the party, and it is her kitten, ZOE, which is the focal point of the laughter. It is lapping away at a pint glass of bitter.

CHRIS: Will she be on the tiles tonight!

Another roar of laughter. (They are obviously in a state where they'd laugh at anything – even themselves).

Mike enters and stands in the doorway trying to decide which is the easiest way to the bar. He starts to push his way to the bar. There is another roar of laughter from the semi-circle. MIKE jostles a heavily made-up GIRL, spilling her drink slightly. MIKE mumbles an apology. SELBY BROOKS looks up from the kitten, seeing MIKE. She watches him with languid interest as he continues on his way to the bar.

As he gets to the bar, MIKE tries to attract the attention of the BARMAID, without success. She is being run off her feet.

SELBY rises and makes her way to the bar and MIKE.

BOB WEST, the landlord, comes in from the other bar and takes up a bottle of Scotch. He is fifty-five years old, not a crook, but not averse to making a fast buck.

MIKE: Have you got a telephone I could use?

WEST: (*Cutting MIKE short*) All in good time, Mac!

MIKE: I've had trouble with my car and I want to phone
             …

WEST: (*It is a heavy evening*) I've only got five pairs of
             hands!

SELBY appears a little behind MIKE at the bar as BOB WEST goes back into the other bar with the bottle of Scotch. MIKE sighs irritatedly, and turns, jogging SELBY as he does so.

MIKE: Oh – I'm terribly sorry.

SELBY smiles enigmatically and indicates that MIKE follow her with the barest nod of the head and starts to push her way through the crowd once more. MIKE glances a little uneasily from side to side, then follows her. As he does so, the group's musician – an untidy young man with a guitar – starts to play. LOUIS DUBINSKY is standing next to the guitarist. He is following SELBY and MIKE's progress through the crowd with interest.

SELBY reaches the wall of the bar and glances behind to see that MIKE is following, then she opens a door in the wall. This door is not immediately noticeable, being covered in the wallpaper of the room. She goes through the doorway. MIKE reaches the doorway, hesitates, glancing around him, then quickly follows SELBY through the door.

CUT TO: A Narrow Staircase leading upstairs. Evening.
This is immediately on the other side of the doorway from the bar.
SELBY is ascending the stairs. She glances back at MIKE who stands there looking up at her. She continues on up the stairway. MIKE closes the door and follows her.

CUT TO: SELBY's Room at The Fourposter. Evening.
This is a large room with heavy Victorian pieces. But SEL has occupied it for some time and had lightened the atmosphere considerably. There are several "throw the brush at the canvas" paintings (by CHRIS BENSON), Quatermass-looking sculptures, a record-player, upright piano, and a divan bed. The cover on the divan has a kitten motif, made of the same material as SEL's blouse.
SEL enters the room and turns to look at MIKE who remains hesitantly in the doorway. SEL smiles faintly and indicates the telephone on the sideboard.
MIKE: Oh – thanks.
MIKE, still looking vaguely at SEL, moves to the telephone. Suddenly, there is the frightened mewing of cats. MIKE starts

17

and looks down. Two cats belt in fright from their saucer of milk. MIKE looks apologetically at SEL.

MIKE: I'm sorry. I didn't see them.

SEL smiles faintly and moves to the divan, half lying down on it and stroking the kitten she is carrying. MIKE looks awkwardly at SEL. He turns to the telephone, collects his thoughts, having almost forgotten what he is telephoning about. He dials the number. SEL continues stroking the kitten and smiling as she watches MIKE.

MIKE: (*On the phone*) Hello? … Is that the A.A.? … Look – my car's packed up and I'm stuck in the middle of the King's Road, Chelsea … Hilton – Mike Hilton … 761 GPD … Thanks … I'll give you a ring later from the Dorchester … Goodbye.

MIKE replaces the receiver and looks at SEL, putting his hand in his pocket for his money.

MIKE: Thanks very much …

SEL: Have that one on the house.

MIKE: Oh no, please! It was very kind of you …

MIKE smiles awkwardly and places the money on the sideboard. SEL glances down at the kitten. MIKE goes to the divan, hesitates, then strokes the kitten. SEL raises her eyes, looking up at him. Their eyes hold for a brief moment. The kitten jumps down.

MIKE: Well, thank you again, Miss – ?

SEL is still looking at MIKE as she rises slowly from the divan.

SEL: Brooks. Selby Brooks.

SEL turns away, moving to the door.

CUT TO: The Fourposter. Saloon Bar. Evening.

The GUITARIST is warming up now and playing his full range (four chords). The others are clapping their hands, snapping their fingers, humming, singing, clinking beer glances, and voodoo drumming the tabletops. DUBINSKY suddenly stops beating time to the music as he sees SEL and MIKE come through the door and into the bar.

MIKE: (*As he and SEL come through the door in the wall*)
          Well – thanks again. It was really awfully kind of
          you. Goodbye.

SEL merely smiles and picks up the kitten which has suddenly appeared again. MIKE hesitates, then goes.

CUT TO: The Kings's Road. Chelsea. Day.

About half a mile from The Fourposter; the Sloane Square end.
It is a Saturday afternoon. It is busy and the traffic is thick.

MIKE's car is crawling along in the traffic congestion with MIKE at the wheel, alone in the car. He is wearing sports clothes and looks tired and irritated. His golf clubs are on the back seat. He casually glances across at the pavement and the milling pedestrians – suddenly he "double-takes". SELBY BROOKS, dressed as we first saw her, is coming out of a store. She carries a shopping bag – the kitten peeps out over the top of the bag.

MIKE brakes just in time to avoid running into the car in front. He calls out to SEL.

MIKE: Hello, there!

SELBY turns, recognises MIKE, smiles, and goes to the car. They exchange greetings, MIKE opens the car door and SEL gets in.

CUT TO: Inside MIKE's Car. Day.

MIKE takes off the brake and moves slowly forward. SELBY puts down her shopping bag and lifts out the kitten.

SEL: Will this be quicker than walking?

MIKE: (*Smiling*) I very much doubt it. Are you in a
          hurry?

SEL: Not particularly.

MIKE: Good.

19

MIKE is looking at SEL now.

SEL: Look out!

For a second time, MIKE brakes just in time. They relax and smile at each other. MIKE tickles the neck of the kitten.

CUT TO: The King's Road. Chelsea. Day.

The sports car, with MIKE and SELBY in it, is crawling along. LOUIS DUBINSKY and CHRIS BENSON appear from one of the side streets. DUBINSKY is carrying several secondhand books and CHRIS a large canvas. SELBY waves to the two men as the car suddenly gathers speed. DUBINSKY and CHRIS turn, puzzled – not immediately recognising SELBY; then they realise who it is in the car and wave back. DUBINSKY says something to CHRIS and the artist laughs.

CUT TO: The Fourposter. Chelsea. Day.

MIKE's car pulls up outside The Fourposter.

MIKE: Here we are.

MIKE looks at SEL, then tickles the kitten affectionately.

SEL: Thanks for the lift. (*To the kitten*) That was a nice birthday present, wasn't it, Zoe?

MIKE: It's your birthday?

SEL: Yes.

MIKE: Well – many happy returns.

SEL: I'm giving a party this evening if you'd like to come.

MIKE hesitates. SEL smiles.

SEL: Thanks again for the lift.

SEL makes to get out. MIKE quickly leans over her to open the door, then takes her shopping bag while she gets out.

SEL: Thank you.

MIKE: (*Handing SEL her shopping bag*) About the party – yes, I would like to come.

SELBY smiles.

20

SEL: (*To the kitten*) We'll look forward to seeing
                    you, won't we, Zoe? (*Smiling at MIKE*) Any
                    time after nine. Goodbye.
MIKE makes to say goodbye, but the door is already closed.
He watches SEL from the car as she goes into The Fourposter.

CUT TO: SELBY's Room at The Fourposter. Night.
It is ten o'clock and the party is in full swing. There is no sign
of MIKE. But a great many people have arrived, and the air is
almost as thick as the conversation. CHRIS BENSON, the
artist, is arguing with a MASCULINE WOMAN in a corner. A
crew-cut TEENAGER in a vivid sweater is at the piano giving a
discordant impression of his favourite jazz pianist. The
GUITAR PLAYER, seen earlier, stands nearby playing the
same old four chords. A fashionably MELANCHOLIC PAIR,
wearing their best party depressions, lie on the floor listing off
the people who pain them most, from Picasso to Chan Canasta.
SEL is seated on the divan stroking her cat and talking to an art
shop owner, who at fifty-odd is the 'Daddy' of the party. RUBY
STEVENSON is telling jokes that died twenty years ago to a
group in another corner of the room. IRIS and VIDA, the two
young call-girls, are lounging on the divan, talking and
drinking. They have both kicked off their shoes. DUBINSKY,
the Pole, is the only mobile figure. He is crossing from the
drinks table to SELBY with a tray of drinks. SEL takes a drink,
murmurs thanks, and half smiles up at him.
DUBINSKY: What's happened to that respectable friend of
                    yours?
SEL looks quizzical.
DUBINSKY: Surely you invited him?
SEL laughs.
SEL: Yes, I invited him.
DUBINSKY looks at SEL and smiles.
DUBINSKY: He must have changed his mind.

21

At that moment, BOB WEST calls (from out of shot)

WEST: (*Off*) Sel!

DUBINSKY looks in the direction of the door. WEST has just brought MIKE into the room. MIKE is dressed in a dark suit and white shirt. He is carrying a large box of chocolates. The MELANCHOLIC PAIR are lying on the floor in the foreground looking balefully at MIKE as if he is a creature from another planet. MIKE sees SEL and gives her a slight wave of the hand.

WEST: (*To MIKE, not very helpfully*) Enjoy yourself.

As WEST turns towards the door, SEL rises from the divan with a quick smile of triumph. She dumps Zoe (the kitten) into Dubinsky's arms and goes to MIKE.

CUT TO: SELBY's Room at The Fourposter. Night.

The party is now at its 'wild' height. The musicians have changed instruments. The GUITAR PLAYER is now playing the piano, and the CREW-CUT YOUTH, seated cross-legged on top of the piano, is playing the guitar. RUBY is standing (just about) near the piano, singing with them. MIKE, relaxed in the atmosphere by this time, is sitting on the divan, talking to SEL. She has opened the chocolates and is offering them to him. The MELANCHOLIC PAIR haven't budged an inch and are now in the depths of depression. The MASCULINE WOMAN is dancing with the middle-aged ART DEALER, and other couples, as if glued together, gyrate slowly in a darker corner of the room. IRIS and VIDA are holding an animated conversation with LOUIS DUBINSKY. CHRIS BENSON, the artist, has apparently already left the party.

A long, loud discord at the piano, topped by the raucous voice of RUBY, finishes the number. DUBINSKY turns and gives two slow claps. No one else cares. RUBY, determined to keep the part going, tears over to MIKE and drags him to his feet.

RUBY: Come on! Your turn …

MIKE: Me? But I can't sing …

22

RUBY: Well, you've got to do something! (*To the room*)
          Got to do something, hasn't he?

MIKE looks helplessly at SEL, who is glaring at RUBY.

RUBY: Everybody's got to do a turn … Come on, don't be
          a sour puss! Just to please dear old Ruby! Got to
          do something!

*MIKE sees SEL's expression and decides it is best to fall in
with the tipsy RUBY. He picks up a newspaper from the settee
and flourishes it in the direction of the piano. The GUITAR
PLAYER plays a rolling chord and RUBY claps loudly. MIKE
bows to a puzzled SEL and proceeds to tear the newspaper to
music accompaniment. SEL watches MIKE. The puzzled
expression disappears, and a warm, gentle smile takes its
place.*

*Everyone is watching MIKE now; he finishes tearing the
newspaper and reveals a row of dancing figures. There is a
dramatic chord on the piano, followed by general laughter and
applause (interspersed with good-humoured cries of "Corn"
from IRIS and VIDA). RUBY, delighted by MIKE's unexpected
success, sidles up to him.*

RUBY: Shut up, everybody! (*To MIKE*) Very good, dear.
          Know any other tricks?

*SEL realises that RUBY has taken a liking to MIKE and before
he has time to reply she takes hold of his arm.*

SEL: I'd like a breath of fresh air.

MIKE: So would I. Oh – mustn't forget Zoe.

*MIKE takes up ZOE from the divan. SEL gives RUBY a hard,
meaning look, then smiles at MIKE as he gives her the kitten.
They move to the door.*

CUT TO: The narrow staircase. Night.

*CHRIS BENSON bounds up the stairs with a quart bottle of
beer in either hand. As he reaches SELBY's room door, SEL
and MIKE come out. CHRIS stands aside with mocking*

23

gallantry, bowing and waving the beer bottles. SEL gives him a quick, darting glance, and goes down the stairs, followed by MIKE.

CUT TO: The Fourposter. Saloon Bar. Night.
The pub is empty, as it is after hours. SEL and MIKE come through the staircase door into the bar and are moving to the street door when INGRID, the Swedish blonde, and PETER LLOYD, the second-hand car salesman, come through the door from the other bar. LLOYD is pleasantly drunk.

LLOYD: (*To SEL*) Hello, kitten! Party not over, I hope?
SEL: No. We're just popping out for some air.
MIKE recognises LLOYD.
MIKE: Good evening …
LLOYD: Good … (*Suddenly; recognising MIKE*) Hello, old boy! Didn't recognise you! What a clot! Of course – that's your car outside!
MIKE grins.
MIKE: That's right.
LLOYD: How's it going? Did old Nigel put it right for you?
MIKE: Yes. It's going like a bomb.
LLOYD: I'll bet!
INGRID: Ni-gel? What is this Nigel?
LLOYD: Nigel Green – used to be a racing driver. Got his fingers in all sorts of pies. Cunning old fox! (*Patting INGRID on the bottom*) Not your cup of vodka, Sweetie-Pie …
SEL takes MIKE's arm; she is anxious to go.
SEL: See you later.
INGRID nods. LLOYD waves as MIKE and SELBY move to the street door.
LLOYD: (*To INGRID*) Didn't know you were bringing me to this place! Have I got to climb all these ruddy stairs?

24

INGRID and LLOYD move to the staircase door.

CUT TO: Chelsea Embankment. Night.
SEL is seated on the Embankment wall, holding ZOE, the kitten. MIKE leans on the wall, looking up at her. It is a quiet, mellow evening. In the distance can be seen the stretch of the river and the lights of Battersea Power Station.

SEL: … My mother and father were killed in the Blitz. I have a brother but he went to Canada and I never hear from him.

MIKE: Do you like living in Chelsea – at the pub?
SEL shrugs non-committally.

SEL: It's all right. It's free – it doesn't cost me anything. (*Explaining*) Bob West is my uncle …

MIKE: Oh …

SEL: He's a widower and – well, he's pretty good to me. I help him out in the bars, and he lets me do what I want the rest of the time. But what about you?

MIKE: What about me?

SEL: Are you married?

MIKE: (*After a moment; quietly*) Yes – I'm married.

SEL: (*Amused*) You don't sound very definite about it.

MIKE: We're – not together at the moment. My wife left me about three weeks ago.

SEL: Oh, I'm sorry. (*Not quite sure what to say*) What happened?

MIKE: I don't know what happened. We'd been married ten years. We were very happy, then suddenly –   it just blew up.

SEL: There must have been a reason.
MIKE shrugs; he doesn't wish to pursue the topic.

SEL: (*Lightly*) Perhaps she didn't understand you?

25

MIKE: (*A touch of bitterness*) Oh, she understood me all right. I'm a pretty easy guy to understand. Two easy lessons, a spot of homework, and you know the lot.

SEL: (*Laughing*) I've heard that before.

MIKE and SEL look at each other for a moment. MIKE is faintly embarrassed.

MIKE: It's a nice evening.

SEL: Yes.

MIKE: You're not cold up there, are you?

SEL shakes her head.

SEL: (*Suddenly*) Mike, where do you live? In Town?

MIKE: No, I've got a house in Belford-on-Thames.

SEL: Oh, I know Belford. It's in Surrey – about five miles from Farndale.

MIKE: That's right.

SEL: A friend of mine lives in Farndale. I go down there quite a lot.

MIKE: It's nice this time of the year.

SEL: Yes. (*A moment*) I'm going down on Tuesday, as a matter of fact. (*Smiling at MIKE*) I suppose you wouldn't like to run me there in that heavenly car of yours?

MIKE: Well … (*Suddenly, smiling back at SEL*) I can't think of anything I'd like better.

SEL: Then that's a date.

MIKE nods.

MIKE: Tuesday. I'll pick you up at three o'clock.

SEL: Three o'clock.

MIKE and SEL look at each other again.

SEL: You know, it is getting a bit cold. Let's go back, shall we?

MIKE helps SEL down from the wall. They are close for a moment. MIKE holds her a fraction of a second longer than is necessary.

CUT TO: Houseboat Site. Day.
SEL walks quickly to the gangplank of the houseboat and boards it. MIKE, still puzzled, but now a little amused, follows her.

CUT TO: The Deck of the Houseboat. Day.
SEL smiles mischievously at MIKE as he joins her.

MIKE: You never told me your friend lived on a houseboat.

SEL: You never asked me.

SEL goes through the hatchway door which leads down to the main room of the houseboat. Mike follows her.

CUT TO: The Main Room of the Houseboat. Day.
MIKE and SEL enter the room. It is well equipped and contains among other furnishings a large divan bed and an elaborate Japanese cocktail cabinet. MIKE gives an amused shudder on seeing this ornate abomination. SEL sees his reaction and smiles.

SEL: Isn't it awful? But I'm afraid Miriam likes that sort of thing.

MIKE: This friend of yours – what did you say her name was?

SEL: Miriam Jordan …

MIKE: Does she live here?

SEL: Yes.

MIKE: I mean – permanently?

SEL: (*Amused*) Yes, I know what you mean. She owns the houseboat. She bought it about two years ago.

27

MIKE: Oh. (*Looking around and obviously disliking what he sees*) Well, it's – it's very nice.

SEL: (*Laughing at MIKE*) You think it's ghastly, don't you?

MIKE: (*Faintly embarrassed*) Me, no, I don't. I think it's very cosy.

SEL: Well, I like it, anyway. (*Stretching her arms; obviously pleased with life*) And I'm very grateful to Miriam for letting me come down here whenever I feel like it. It's lovely to get away from the pub sometimes.

MIKE: Yes, I can imagine that.

SEL indicates the cocktail cabinet.

SEL: Help yourself to a drink.

MIKE: But what about your friend? Isn't she …?

SEL: Oh, didn't I tell you? Miriam's not here – she's away – she's in hospital, poor darling.

MIKE: In hospital?

SEL: Yes. They rushed her into St Thomas' on Monday morning. She's got to have an operation.

MIKE: Oh, I'm sorry about that. Is it serious?

SEL: I don't think so. I think it's appendix. Anyway, I've promised to look after the place until she comes out.

MIKE: How long will that be?

SEL shrugs.

SEL: I don't know. How long is an appendix? Ten days – a fortnight?

MIKE: Yes, about ten days.

SEL makes herself comfortable on the divan.

SEL: Pour me a drink, Mike.

MIKE hesitates, then turns towards the cocktail cabinet. He opens it, revealing drinks, glasses, and a built-in glass clock.

SEL: I'll have a gin and tonic.

MIKE mixes the drinks. A large ginger cat suddenly appears, as if from nowhere. (It has actually pushed its way through the half open kitchen door which is on the other side of the room)

MIKE: Hello! What's this – another friend of yours?

SEL laughs.

SEL: That's Ginger … Miriam's cat … Hello, Ginger, where have you been?

SEL picks up the cat and fondles it.

SEL: Now don't fret, Ginger … There's nothing to worry about … Everything's going to be all right, honey …

MIKE smiles and crosses to MEL with her drink.

SEL: (*Taking the glass*) Thanks, darling. What are you having?

MIKE: Oh – I'll have a gin and something.

MIKE returns to the cocktail cabinet. SEL fondles the cat.

SEL: Mike …

MIKE: (*Mixing his drink*) Yes?

SEL: You're an estate agent, aren't you?

MIKE: Yes, I am. Not that you'd notice it these days.

SEL: Well, tell me – what would you pay for a houseboat like this?

MIKE turns, surprised by the question.

MIKE: What – me?

SEL: (*Laughing*) No, I don't mean you in particular … anyone …

MIKE looks around with a faintly professional air as he sips his drink.

MIKE: Oh, it's difficult to say … Fifteen hundred – two thousand, perhaps …

SEL: Yes, that's what I thought.

MIKE moves down to the divan.

MIKE: Why? Are you thinking of buying one?

SEL: I wish I could …

MIKE smiles; he raises his glass.

MIKE: Skol!

SEL: Cheers!

They drink and after a moment, MIKE sits on the divan.

SEL: I've never stayed here before without Miriam. I
                don't know what it'll be like.

*SEL is looking steadily at MIKE as he turns to her, drink in
hand. Their eyes hold for a moment. SEL lowers her eyes,
stroking the cat as she continues in a low voice.*

SEL: It could be rather lonely, I imagine – especially
                at weekends.

MIKE: (*Seemingly weekend thinking*) It needn't be.

*SEL looks quickly up at MIKE. MIKE, as if suddenly aware of
his own words, shifts his attention to the cat. But SEL's gaze
forces him to look at her once again. The look holds.*

CUT TO: Tall Trees. MIKE's Dressing Room. Day.

*This is a small room leading off the main bedroom and
furnished with a man's compactum, wash basin, etc.*

*MIKE is busy packing a weekend case when his housekeeper,
MRS CLIFF, enters the room with the morning mail. She is a
pleasant looking woman in her late fifties.*

MRS CLIFF: The post's just arrived, Mr Hilton.

MRS CLIFF hands MIKE several letters and a postcard.

MIKE: Oh, thank you, Mrs Cliff.

MRS CLIFF: Will you be in to dinner this evening, sir?

MIKE: No, I'm going away for the weekend. I'll be
                back on Monday morning.

*MRS CLIFF nods and goes out. MIKE casually glances at the
letters, which are mostly bills – then with a start he recognises
his wife's familiar handwriting on the postcard. We see that the
postcard reads:*

"Dear Mike,

I arrived in Paris yesterday. Marcel has given me my old job back. Would you please send album in top drawer of dressing table.

Ruth"

CUT TO: Tall Trees. The Bedroom. Day.
MIKE comes out of the dressing room holding the postcard. Obviously a shade puzzled by the message he crosses to RUTH's dressing table and opens the top drawer. There are a few odds and ends in the drawer and a small photograph album with RUTH's initials on it. MIKE hasn't seen the album before, and he opens it with obvious curiosity. The book is full of holiday snaps taken a couple of years ago when their daughter was alive. Scotland. Cornwall. Winter sports in Switzerland. The South of France. He replaces the book in the drawer, knowing full well the effect it will have on him – then suddenly, irresistibly, he picks it up again. He stands by the dressing table, quietly looking at the photographs, slowly turning the pages of the album.

CUT TO: Tall Trees. Surrey. Day.
MIKE's car turns out of the drive onto the main road.

CUT TO: A Country Road. Day.
MIKE is slowly driving along the road by the side of the common. He is deep in thought – thinking of his wife, and of his assignation with SELBY BROOKS. Suddenly, a stone hurtles across the bonnet of the car, missing the windscreen by inches, and striking the off-side wing mirror. MIKE brakes, bringing the car to an immediate standstill. He jumps out of the car and examines the mirror; the glass is broken but no other damage has been done. He looks in the direction of the common.

A wide-eyed nine-year-old BOY in short trousers and a pullover stands staring at MIKE. The BOY is obviously frightened. MIKE walks across to him.

MIKE: Did you throw that stone?

BOY: (*Nervously*) Yes, sir. I'm very sorry, I didn't mean to hit your car.

MIKE: Well – what did you mean to do?

The BOY points towards one of the trees.

BOY: I was trying to get my kite down …

MIKE looks across to where the BOY is pointing. He sees the kite firmly lodged in the top branches of the tree. He looks down at the BOY again.

MIKE: You should be more careful.

BOY: Yes, sir.

MIKE turns and is about to return to his car, then hesitates. He looks up at the kite.

MIKE: How long's it been up there?

BOY: I – I don't know …

MIKE: (*Aggressively; but not unfriendly*) You don't know?

BOY: (*Nervously; near to tears*) No – no, sir.

MIKE stands looking at the boy; suddenly he smiles and the BOY, obviously relieved, smiles back at him.

MIKE: It looks a very nice kite. Did your father buy it for you?

BOY: Yes, and he'll be very cross if I lose it.

MIKE: Then you mustn't lose it, must you? (*He pats the boy's head*) Don't worry, we'll get it down. They used to call me Slinger at school.

BOY: Slinger?

MIKE: Yes, I was a pot shot with a sling, you see. (*He glances at his watch*) Get me some ammunition, old man. Anything'll do. Pebbles, stones, bricks, twigs.

32

The BOY's smile broadens, the last of his anxiety removed now. He goes in search of pebbles for MIKE to throw at the tree.

CUT TO: The Tree with the Kite lodged in its branches.

A stone thrown from behind the camera rustles the branches. The kite agitates but remains stubbornly in its position. MIKE is standing in his shirt-sleeves, weighing another stone in his hand.

The BOY stands mute and still a few yards away, MIKE's jacket in one hand and the kite string in the other. (The string is no longer attached to the kite.) Needless to say, the BOY's anxiety has returned. MIKE looks at him.

MIKE: I have to be careful, you see, otherwise I might hit the kite.

The BOY is not wholly convinced. MIKE, with fanatical concentration, throws the stone into the tree. The BOY watches the flight of it with little or no hope. He looks at MIKE. MIKE smiles wryly.

MIKE: They wouldn't call me Slinger in your school, I know.

The BOY manages a smile. MIKE sighs, puts his hands on his hips, and looks up at the kite. He weighs up the height from the ground.

MIKE: Well, there's only one thing for it. Here we go.

MIKE spits on his hands and runs towards the tree. He springs up, catching the lowest branch and hauling himself up to a sitting position on it. He looks up at the next branch. He is not too sure how to reach it. He looks down at the BOY and forces a smile, then he cautiously stands up and determinedly starts to climb.

He reaches the branch in which the kite is lodged. He shakes the branch, but the kite does not budge. MIKE works his way cautiously along the branch.

The BOY has put MIKE's jacket and the string on the ground now. He watches MIKE anxiously, not so much concerned about the kite at the moment.

MIKE is within a foot or so of the kite now. He reaches forward and flicks it. He flicks it a second time and the kite falls to the ground. The BOY runs delightedly towards it. MIKE looks down. He smiles to himself. The delight on the boy's face has been worth the climb.

CUT TO: MIKE and the BOY.

MIKE is just putting on his jacket. The BOY has just finished re-tying the string to the kite. He looks at MIKE, his eyes filled with gratitude.

BOY: Sorry it took so long.

MIKE smiles and looks at his watch.

BOY: Is it twelve o'clock yet? My father said he'd be back by twelve.

MIKE: It's a quarter past. My goodness, we've been over half an hour rescuing that kite of yours.

BOY: I'm sorry, sir.

MIKE: ´   That's all right. But don't do it again!

MIKE winks. The BOY smiles and moves out of shot. MIKE starts back to his car, straightening his tie and smoothing back his hair.

CUT TO: The Houseboat Site. Day.

MIKE's car turns out of the lane leading to the site and stops. MIKE sits in the driving seat looking towards the houseboat. He is obviously undecided. After a moment he reaches for the weekend case, which is on the passenger seat. He hesitates – then suddenly his mind is made up. He leaves the case where it is and gets out of the car. He goes from the houseboat, crossing the gangplank onto the deck.

CUT TO: The Deck of the Houseboat. Day.
MIKE crosses to the hatchway and disappears down the steps which lead to the living quarters.

CUT TO: The Door of the Main Room of the Houseboat. Day.
MIKE is about to open the door, then he hesitates – SEL may be changing. He decides to knock. There is no reply. He knocks again. He waits, then goes in.

CUT TO: The Main Room of the Houseboat. Day.
MIKE enters and stops dead, surveying the room in astonishment. There has obviously been a struggle. The cocktail cabinet has been overturned, glasses smashed, the wall mirror broken, etc. MIKE's eyes finally rest on the divan. His eyes widen in horror as he moves automatically towards it. He stops a foot or two away from it. SEL's naked leg protrudes from under the tumbled eiderdown. MIKE is transfixed. Something at his feet arrests his attention. He bends slowly and takes it up. It is SEL's blouse, the one with the kitten motif. It has obviously been torn off SEL during the struggle. MIKE is staring at it when a noise startles him. He drops the blouse and turns sharply, looking at something to the right behind him.
The CAT is perched on a shelf – angry, spitting, full of revenge. It leaps forward and lands on MIKE's shoulder. MIKE half falls onto the divan, instinctively defending himself with his hand. With a desperate movement, he releases himself from the cat's claws and plunges towards the door.
The eiderdown on the divan has been disturbed by MIKE's fall and we now see SEL's face hanging over the edge of the divan – the eyes staring.

CUT TO: Belford-on-Thames Police Station. Day.

The DESK SERGEANT is writing busily as DETECTIVE INSPECTOR CRADDOCK comes out of his office. As they exchange greetings, the telephone rings on the SERGEANT's desk. CRADDOCK moves to the door.

SERGEANT: (*On the phone*) Belford Police Station ... Just one moment. (*Hailing CRADDOCK*) Excuse me, sir – a Mr Hilton for you.

CRADDOCK: Oh, thank you, Sergeant. (*Taking the phone*) Inspector Craddock here – good afternoon, sir ...

CRADDOCK listens for a moment or two, then his expression changes.

CRADDOCK: No – stay where you are, sir! We'll be right over!

CUT TO: The Deck of the Houseboat. Day.

Several police cars are parked on the site and a DETECTIVE is examining the gang-plank. MIKE is on the deck, smoking a cigarette. His hand is bandaged with a handkerchief. He looks anxiously at the hatchway leading down to the main room of the houseboat.

CUT TO: The Main Room of the Houseboat. Day.

CRADDOCK is looking thoughtfully at the body of SEL. A POLICE DOCTOR is just putting his things into his bag, having finished his examination of the body. FLASH! – As a POLICE PHOTOGRAPHER takes a picture. A FINGERPRINT MAN is at work on the overturned cocktail cabinet. A DETECTIVE SERGEANT stands near him.

DOCTOR: (*To CRADDOCK*) Well, do you want me to blind you with science or give it to you straight?

CRADDOCK: Let's have it straight, Doctor. Save the big words for the Coroner.

DOCTOR: Right. She's been strangled.

CRADDOCK: (*Quickly*) When?

DOCTOR: (*Smiling*) Yes, I thought you'd want me to stick my neck out. She's been dead about an hour and a half; two hours, perhaps.

The SERGEANT indicates the broken clock in the cocktail cabinet.

SERGEANT: That ties up with the clock …

DOCTOR: (*To SERGEANT*) What time does the clock say?

SERGEANT: (*Kneeling down by the cabinet*) … Six minutes to twelve …

The DOCTOR nods.

DOCTOR: Yes, I should think that's about when it happened. (*Glancing around the room*) My God, she certainly put up a struggle!

CRADDOCK says nothing; he looks at his wristlet watch.

CUT TO: The Deck of the Houseboat. Day.

MIKE is now standing a few yards from the hatchway. He tosses his cigarette end into the water. The DOCTOR suddenly appears, glances across at MIKE, and crosses to the gangplank towards his car. CRADDOCK comes out after him. He looks at MIKE then goes over to him.

CRADDOCK: … Tell me about Miss Brooks, sir. How long have you known her?

MIKE: About two weeks. My car broke down on the way to Town one night and I had to telephone … (*Hesitantly; tensely*) Inspector, what's happened?

CRADDOCK: There was a struggle – a pretty desperate one by the look of things – and she was strangled.

MIKE: (*Softly*) Good God … What sort of a man would do a thing like that?

CRADDOCK: (*Quietly*) Go on, sir – tell me about Miss Brooks. Does she own this houseboat?

MIKE: No, it belongs to a friend of hers who's having an operation. Miriam Jordan, I think she said her name was. She's in St Thomas'.

CRADDOCK nods.

MIKE: Sel – Miss Brooks – was looking after it for her.

CRADDOCK: I see. And you've been here before, I take it?

MIKE: Yes, once before – last Tuesday.

CRADDOCK: And how long did you stay on that occasion?

MIKE: Oh, about five or ten minutes. We had a drink and arranged to meet this morning – for lunch. I was supposed to pick her up at twelve o'clock.

CRADDOCK: Did you get here at twelve o'clock, sir?

MIKE: No, I was late.

CRADDOCK: How late?

MIKE: Oh, I didn't arrive until about ten to one.

CRADDOCK: Why was that?

MIKE: A boy hit my car with a stone, and I stayed to give him a piece of my mind. I finished up by rescuing his kite. It was caught in a tree.

CRADDOCK: (*Curious*) Where was this, exactly?

MIKE: Oh – now what do they call that place? That little common just past Farndale?

CRADDOCK: Oh, I know it, sir. I know the spot you mean. Go on …

MIKE: Well, I thought it was going to be dead easy – getting the kite down, I mean. It took me over half an hour.

38

CRADDOCK: That seems rather a long time. Are you sure it was that long?

MIKE: Yes, I'm quite sure. It was about twenty to twelve when the boy spoke to me, and I know it was a quarter past when I left him.

CRADDOCK: You seem very definite about the time, sir.

MIKE: I am definite. I looked at my watch. In any case, if the time's important the boy will confirm it. He asked me the time just before I left him.

CRADDOCK: (*Quietly*) What time do you make it now, sir?

MIKE looks at CRADDOCK, then realises the point of the question and shows CRADDOCK his watch. The INSPECTOR nods.

CRADDOCK: Was anyone else on the common – while you were with the boy?

MIKE: I didn't see anyone.

CRADDOCK: I presume he was one of the local children, since he was on his own?

MIKE: (*Faintly on edge*) I don't know, I imagine so. I'd never seen him before.

CRADDOCK: Did he tell you his name, sir?

MIKE: No, I'm afraid he didn't.

CRADDOCK takes a notebook out of his inside pocket.

CRADDOCK: Give me a description of him.

MIKE: (*Agitated*) Look, Inspector – surely this isn't important, about the boy and the kite?

CRADDOCK: It could be very important, Mr Hilton.

MIKE stares at the INSPECTOR; he is puzzled now as well as worried.

CUT TO: The Country Road. Day.

MIKE's car is driving slowly past the common, the area where he met the boy. There is no sign of the boy with the kite. MIKE is at the wheel, looking searchingly out of the car window. He reacts to seeing something. In the distance a BOY and a GIRL are playing ball with a NURSEMAID. A pram is nearby.

MIKE stops the car and gets out. He goes to the NURSEMAID, BOY and GIRL and speaks to the NURSEMAID; she shakes her head and speaks to the children. They look at MIKE, shaking their heads. MIKE thanks them and returns to his car. He gets into the driving seat and sits there staring out thoughtfully at the common. He looks distinctly worried as he starts the car.

CUT TO: A Children's Playground. Belford-on-Thames. Day.

A group of CHILDREN are playing in a tree-lined playground adjoining the local park. A police car very slowly drives past the playground. A worried looking MIKE sits in the front seat, next to the UNIFORMED DRIVER. He has a sticking plaster on his hand. MIKE carefully scans the faces of the children, then looks at the driver and slowly shakes his head.

CUT TO: The Classroom of A Secondary Modern School near Belford-on-Thames. Day.

A rather gaunt looking MAN in rimless glasses is endeavouring to explain a mathematical problem to a class of about twenty restless BOYS. He is interrupted by the arrival of MIKE and a PLAIN-CLOTHES DETECTIVE SERGEANT. The SERGEANT nods to the teacher and the lesson continues. MIKE stands just inside the classroom surveying the boys. After a little while he looks at the SERGEANT and shakes his head. The SERGEANT opens the door, giving a nod of thanks to the teacher as they go out.

CUT TO: A Room at Belford-on-Thames Police Station. Day.

MIKE is sitting at a table carefully examining a large photograph through a magnifying glass. This is a group photograph, taken at a local school. He is studying each figure separately, with the aid of the magnifying glass, in the hope of finding the boy with the kite. Numerous photographs of all shapes and sizes are scattered across the table. A UNIFORMED POLICEMAN enters carrying another batch of photographs and a copy of the Evening News.

POLICEMAN: Any luck?

MIKE: No …

POLICEMAN: Well, I've brought you some more. (*He puts the photographs down*) These are from private schools … Oh, and I thought you might like to see this, sir.

The POLICEMAN puts the newspaper down on the table. MIKE turns from the photograph to look at the paper. The banner headline reads: "POLICE SEEK 'KITE' BOY"

CUT TO: INSPECTOR CRADDOCK's Office. Belford-on-Thames. Day.

This is an untidy office, furnished with the usual plain wooden desk, steel cupboards, and filing cabinets.

ALICE THORPE, a determined, self-possessed District Nurse, is sitting opposite INSPECTOR CRADDOCK who is behind the desk. CHIEF SUPERINTENDENT O'DAY occupies a chair on the INSPECTOR's right.

O'DAY: … I still don't understand why you didn't go down to the houseboat?

ALICE: I've explained why! I was on my way to a confinement, and I was late.

O'DAY: Yes, but surely, when you hear someone shouting for help …

ALICE: I didn't hear anyone shouting for help! Please don't twist my words, Superintendent! I simply said I heard voices. It could have meant anything …

41

O'DAY: In this particular instance it meant that a girl was being murdered.

ALICE: (*Indignantly*) And how was I to know that? I'm not a thought reader ...

CRADDOCK: (*Pacifying ALICE*) Anyway, you're sure – quite sure – about the time?

ALICE: I'm positive. It was just after ten minutes to twelve.

CRADDOCK nods and rises.

CRADDOCK: Thank you, Sister – you've been a great help.

ALICE: I'm glad someone thinks so.

The INSPECTOR opens the door and with a look at O'DAY ALICE goes out.

O'DAY: (*Rising*) ... Snooty little devil ... Still, I think she's reliable. There's no doubt about the time; we can be sure of that now. It must have happened as near twelve as damn it.

CRADDOCK: Yes; which lets out Mike Hilton – once we find the boy.

O'DAY: Once we find him. (*Sitting on the corner of the desk*) You don't think Hilton did it, do you, Craddock?

CRADDOCK: No, I don't. I've known Mike Hilton for years.

O'DAY: Do you know his wife?

CRADDOCK: I've met her.

O'DAY: I understand she's left him.

CRADDOCK: (*Cautiously*) Yes, I've heard that rumour.

O'DAY: It's more than a rumour. She's in Paris, working for a travel agency. (*The INSPECTOR makes no comment*) What was the trouble, Craddock? Was he playing around?

CRADDOCK: No. No, I'm sure it wasn't anything like that.

O'DAY: Well, what was it?

CRADDOCK: I don't know. I think perhaps things have been a little … (*He hesitates*) difficult for them just recently.

O'DAY: Difficult? (*Picking up a folder from the desk*) In what way? He's not exactly on the bread line.

CRADDOCK: I didn't mean that. They had a child; a little girl. About a year ago she caught pneumonia and died. Hilton took it very badly, I'm afraid.

A UNIFORMED SERGEANT enters.

CRADDOCK: What is it, Roberts?

ROBERTS: Mr Hilton's here, sir.

CRADDOCK: All right, show him in.

ROBERTS goes out.

O'DAY studies the file. CRADDOCK glances at him, then crosses to the window; he stands thoughtfully staring out at the trim little path which leads down to the main road. There is a knock on the door and ROBERTS returns with MIKE.

As the SERGEANT goes out CRADDOCK returns from the window. MIKE is still wearing the sticking plaster on his hand.

CRADDOCK: Good afternoon, Mr Hilton.

MIKE: Good afternoon, Inspector.

CRADDOCK: This is Superintendent O'Day, from Scotland Yard.

MIKE looks at O'DAY who is still reading the contents of the folder.

MIKE: (*Nervously*) How d'you do?

For a brief moment O'DAY ignores MIKE, then he suddenly looks up and smiles.

O'DAY: Hello, Mr Hilton. How's the hand?

MIKE: Oh – it's all right, thanks.

O'DAY: Well, be careful – a scratch like that can be very nasty. I've just been reading your

43

	statement, sir. It makes interesting reading, even if it is a little confusing.
MIKE:	Confusing?
O'DAY:	Yes. You told Inspector Craddock that the houseboat belonged to a woman called Miriam Jordan.
MIKE:	That's right.
O'DAY:	Who gave you that choice piece of information, sir?
MIKE:	Why Sel – Miss Brooks did.
O'DAY:	And you believed her?
MIKE:	*(Amazed)* Of course I believed her!

O'DAY looks at the file.

O'DAY:	The houseboat was bought from Jackson Bros. of Kingston on the third of June last year. The price was sixteen hundred pounds. The purchaser was a Miss Selby Brooks. (*He looks at MIKE*) She paid in cash.
MIKE:	*(Staggered)* I – I don't believe this …
CRADDOCK:	It's true, Mr Hilton, apart from the information from Jackson Bros. we've checked at the hospital. There's no one called Miriam Jordan.
MIKE:	But there must be! I just don't believe that … (*Suddenly, to O'DAY*) Look, this is nonsense about the houseboat! Where would Sel get sixteen hundred pounds?

O'DAY looks at MIKE for a moment and then indicates the armchair.

O'DAY:	Sit down, sir. I think you and I had better have a little chat, Mr Hilton.

MIKE hesitates, then crosses to the chair.

O'DAY:	(*Tapping the folder*) According to this, the first time you went to the Hotbed was just over three weeks ago.

MIKE: The Hotbed?

O'DAY: The pub, sir. The Fourposter. Our local people
               call it the Hotbed. (*Smiling*) Not without a very
               good reason, I assure you.

MIKE looks at O'DAY, then across at CRADDOCK.

MIKE: What are you trying to tell me?

O'DAY: Something you must already know, Mr Hilton.
               Selby Brooks was a bad lot. Just how bad …

MIKE: I don't believe this! I just don't believe a word
               of it!

CRADDOCK: (*Quietly*) What did Miss Brooks tell you about
               herself, sir?

MIKE hesitates, then:

MIKE: She said she lived at The Fourposter with her
               uncle and that he …

O'DAY: (*Surprised*) Her uncle?

MIKE: Yes. Bob West – he's the landlord …

O'DAY: (*Smiling*) Go on, sir.

MIKE: (*Looking at O'DAY*) She said her mother and
               father had been killed in the Blitz.

O'DAY: Her father's alive. He has a draper's shop in
               Bristol. He's a nice, quiet little man – until you
               mention his daughter. What else did she tell
               you?

MIKE: (*Worried; defensively*) Nothing. Nothing at all
               …

O'DAY: Mr Hilton, for some time now we've suspected
               that – quite apart from her other activities –
               Miss Brooks was going in for blackmail.

MIKE: What do you mean – her other activities?

O'DAY: (*With sudden authority*) Don't try and
               bamboozle me, please. You've been friendly
               with this girl. You know what I mean, sir. (*He
               turns and puts the file down on the desk*) Now

	it's my belief that she got friendly with you, borrowed money, and then tried to blackmail you into …
MIKE:	(*Alarmed*) No! No, this isn't true! (*Appealing to CRADDOCK*) This isn't true, Inspector!

O'DAY looks at MIKE, and a shade puzzled by his obvious sincerity decides to change his tactics.

O'DAY:	You told Inspector Craddock that you arrived at the houseboat at about ten minutes to one.
MIKE:	Yes.
O'DAY:	You would have arrived earlier – quite a lot earlier, in fact – but you helped a boy who was in trouble with his kite.
MIKE:	(*Irritated*) Yes.
O'DAY:	Why hasn't this boy come forward?
MIKE:	I don't know.
O'DAY:	Why haven't we heard from either the boy or his parents?
MIKE:	I don't know why. (*Lamely*) Perhaps they don't live near here …
O'DAY:	Wherever they live they must read the newspapers, or listen to the radio, or watch the television. (*Shaking his head*) You know, we've really gone to town on this boy, Mr Hilton – we've really tried to find him for you.
MIKE:	Yes, I know you have and I appreciate it. (*Bewildered; shaking his head*) I just don't understand why he hasn't turned up.
O'DAY:	Neither do I. (*Facing MIKE*) Now tell me about your first visit to the houseboat. (*Politely*) There were only two visits?
MIKE:	(*Making an effort to control himself*) Yes – only two.
O'DAY:	How long did you stay on the first occasion?

MIKE: Look, I've already told Inspector Craddock this
…

O'DAY: (*Unruffled*) Now tell me …

MIKE: Five or ten minutes. We had a drink, that's all.

O'DAY: You didn't entertain Miss Brooks?

MIKE: Entertain her?

O'DAY: Yes, sir. Party tricks. Fun and games.

MIKE: (*Angrily*) Are you trying to be funny? What the
hell are you talking about?

*O'DAY suddenly picks up a newspaper from the desk and opens
it, revealing a paper pattern of dancing figures.*

O'DAY: I'm talking about this, Mr Hilton.

MIKE stares at the newspaper in complete astonishment.

MIKE: Where – did you find that?

O'DAY looks across at the INSPECTOR.

CRADDOCK: On the houseboat.

CUT TO: Outside Belford Police Station. Day.

*A police car is parked near the trim little path leading up to the
Police Station. O'DAY and CRADDOCK are standing near this
car, having a final word before the SUPERINTENDENT
returns to London. A UNIFORMED DRIVER is at the wheel.*

CRADDOCK: … But who did Selby Brooks get the sixteen
hundred pounds from – that's what I'd like to
know? She couldn't have got it from Hilton. He
only met her three weeks ago.

O'DAY: Well, I'll tell you what I think, Craddock.
When the girls were cleared off the streets a
certain gentleman in Chelsea started the call-
girl racket. He was wildly successful; so
successful in fact that we've never been able to
catch up with him. Most of the girls don't know
who he is, they deal with a go-between. The

47

few who do know – (*A shrug*) keep their mouths shut.

CRADDOCK: Well?

O'DAY: It's my bet Selby Brooks met this man and blackmailed him.

CRADDOCK: Then surely, he would have committed the murder?

O'DAY: (*Thoughtfully*) Yes, he would have done.

CRADDOCK: But you don't think he did?

O'DAY: (*Hesitating, then:*) I just don't believe that story of Mike Hilton's about the boy and the kite. I never will believe it. (*He looks at the INSPECTOR*) Unless, of course, you find the boy, Craddock.

O'DAY nods and gets into the car.

CUT TO: DUBINSKY's Bookshop. King's Road. Chelsea. Evening.

LOUIS DUBINSKY is closing his bookshop down for the night; removing trestle boxes of second-hand books and paperbacks which have been on display outside the shop. Unnoticed by DUBINSKY, the blue sports car, with MIKE driving, passes by the shop and continues down the King's Road towards The Fourposter.

CUT TO: The Fourposter. Saloon Bar. Evening.

It is a quiet night. None of the usual crowd are present, apart from RUBY STEVENSON and CHRIS BENSON, the artist, who are talking quietly together in a corner of the room. A man in a blue blazer and grey flannel bags sits at the bar reading a newspaper and munching sandwiches. A new face is behind the bar – round and blonde fringed. MIKE enters, doesn't immediately notice the two in the corner, and crosses to the bar. CHRIS and RUBY have noticed MIKE, however, and

48

*during MIKE's conversation with the BARMAID they give each
other a significant nod and move towards the door.*

BARMAID: Good evening.

MIKE: I'd like a word with Mr West.

BARMAID: (*After a slight hesitation*) He's not here, I'm
            afraid.

MIKE: When will he be back?

BARMAID: Not for a few days. He's not well. That's why
            I'm here.

MIKE: Where has he gone, do you know?

BARMAID: No, I don't.

VOICE: (*Off*) Pint please, Nelly.

BARMAID: (*Abruptly*) I'm sorry, I can't help you. Excuse
            me.

*The BARMAID is glad to get away. MIKE moves as if to speak
to her again, then suddenly notices RUBY and CHRIS.*

MIKE: Ruby!

MIKE crosses to RUBY and CHRIS.

MIKE: I want to talk to you …

RUBY: Can't stop now, Duckie – we're off to the flicks
            and we're late already …

MIKE: (*Taking hold of RUBY's arm*) I'm sorry, but
            I've got to talk to you!

RUBY hesitates; she looks appealingly at CHRIS.

CHRIS: (*Deserting RUBY*) I'll see if I can pick up a cab
            …

CHRIS goes out quickly, leaving an annoyed RUBY with MIKE.

MIKE: (*Indicating a table*) Sit down. I'll get you a
            drink.

RUBY hesitates, then sits at the table.

RUBY: I don't want a drink. I haven't got time.

*MIKE sits opposite RUBY at the table; he leans forward; he is
tense.*

MIKE: You've got to tell me about Sel …

RUBY: I don't want to talk about Sel. It upsets me.

MIKE: Ruby, you've got to talk about her. There are certain things I must know.

RUBY: I was very upset about Sel. Very. The police came round to my place. They questioned me. I suppose you know that?

MIKE: (*Shaking his head*) No …

RUBY: (*Surprised*) Didn't you put them up to it?

MIKE: No, of course I didn't.

RUBY: I thought perhaps you told them I was a friend of hers?

MIKE: No, I never mentioned you. Why should I?

RUBY looks at MIKE, wondering whether he is telling the truth or not. She decides that he is.

RUBY: (*After a moment; cautiously*) What is it you want to know?

MIKE: Did Sel own that houseboat?

RUBY: (*After a momentary hesitation*) Yes.

MIKE: Well – how did she buy it? Where did she get the money from?

RUBY shrugs.

MIKE: The police said she was a blackmailer. Was she?

RUBY: Did she blackmail <u>you</u>?

MIKE: She lied to me. She must have done because …

RUBY: (*Suddenly angry; interrupting MIKE*) Did she blackmail <u>you</u>?

MIKE: (*Quietly*) No. No, she didn't …

RUBY: Did she borrow money from you?

MIKE: No.

RUBY: Did she try to?

MIKE is a little taken aback by RUBY's vehemence.

MIKE: Why, no …

RUBY rises.

RUBY: Then what the hell are you bellyaching about? Judge people as you find them!

RUBY gives MIKE a look and goes out. MIKE sits at the table, obviously surprised by RUBY's outburst. Finally, he rises and crosses to the door. The MAN in a blazer turns and watches him. We recognise this man now – it is DETECTIVE SERGEANT JACK BELLAMY.

CUT TO: NIGEL GREEN's Car Showroom. Belford-on-Thames. Day.

NIGEL GREEN is reading a newspaper. He can see the front page has a photograph of the houseboat and inset photographs of SELBY BROOKS and MIKE. A car can be heard pulling up outside the showroom and, lowering the newspaper, NIGEL sees MIKE getting out of his car. He crosses to the door as MIKE enters.

NIGEL: (*Not quite as affable as usual*) Afternoon, Mike.

MIKE: Hello, Nigel. How's business?

NIGEL: Oh – fair …

MIKE: Nigel, do you remember when I dropped in here a couple of weeks ago – you were talking to a tall, rather sporty looking man …

NIGEL: Check suit; suede shoes? He was looking at an Austin-Healey?

MIKE: That's right …

NIGEL: Peter Lloyd.

MIKE: That's the chap! Where does he live, do you know?

NIGEL: Haven't a clue. He's got one of these open-air places in Shepherd's Bush. Second-hand jobs. He takes a lot of my rougher stuff. You know, people trade it in. Naturally, I daren't sell it down here.

MIKE: I'd like to talk to him if possible.

NIGEL: Well, I don't see why not (*Pulling MIKE's leg, but curious*) Why – are you thinking of doing a swap?
MIKE: Good heavens, no! (*Hesitantly*) I think, perhaps, he might be able to help me.
NIGEL: Oh? In what way?
MIKE: He knew Selby …
NIGEL: Selby?

MIKE indicates the newspaper that NIGEL is holding.

MIKE: Selby Brooks … The girl you've just been reading about.
NIGEL: (*Faintly embarrassed*) Oh … (*Smiling*) Well, that doesn't completely surprise me. Old Peter knows most people; he gets around. I'm seeing him tomorrow night, I'll ask him to give you a ring.
MIKE: Is he coming down here?
NIGEL: No; I've got an M.G. he's interested in. I'm taking it up to Town.
MIKE: Would you mind if I came along?
NIGEL: (*Hesitantly*) Well – you can if you want to.
MIKE: Thanks.
NIGEL: Drop in about eight …

MIKE nods.

CUT TO: A Soho Street. London. Night.
A ten-year-old M.G. driven by NIGEL GREEN, with MIKE in the passenger seat, turns into the street.

CUT TO: A Neon Sign which reads: "NUDE-VU CLUB"

CUT TO: The Nude-Vu Club. London. Night.
A row of lardy, hypnotised faces with dropped jaws and glassy eyes are looking at the stage. A leg peels a stocking to the accompaniment of a breathy Spanish number with a Clapham North accent.

PETER LLOYD is in the gangway seat, looking respectably bored. A uniformed ATTENDANT enters and whispers in LLOYD's ear. LLOYD nods and, still watching the stage, rises and moves along the gangway out of shot.

CUT TO: The Nude-Vu Club Bar. Night.

This is the bar at the back of the club. Opposite the bar counter a curtained doorway leads to the theatre, from which the Spanish number can be heard. A BARMAID who looks as if she could out-bust any of the strippers on stage, is serving NIGEL and MIKE with drinks. MIKE stands awkwardly, glancing around the 'art' panelling on the walls.

NIGEL: (*To the BARMAID*) Thanks, Peg.

MIKE looks faintly surprised at the "Peg".

NIGEL: Doris sounds a bit thick tonight. (*He is alluding to the singer*)

PEG: Got a cold. I told her about leaving her sweater off, but she won't be told.

NIGEL smiles faintly at MIKE. There is scattered applause. The curtains part and LLOYD enters.

LLOYD: Nigel …

NIGEL: Pete – you know Mike Hilton, of course?

LLOYD: Yes, rather. (*His expression is both sympathetic and curious*) How are you? Awfully sorry to hear about that friend of yours. Shocking business. Tough luck, old man. (*To NIGEL*) Got the M.G.?

NIGEL: Yes, it's outside. But Mike wants a quick word with you first.

LLOYD: Oh – really?

NIGEL: Shan't be a tick. Another whisky, Peg. (*He indicates it is for LLOYD*)

A MAN enters as NIGEL goes to the exit; NIGEL smiles and nods to him as he passes. The MAN comes to the bar.

LLOYD: Well – what is it, old boy?

53

MIKE: I thought you might be able to help me …

LLOYD: Of course. What can I do? Any pal of Nigel's …
         (*He leaves it unfinished*)

MIKE: You knew Selby, didn't you?

LLOYD makes to answer, then hesitates as PEG fetches his whisky.

LLOYD: Thanks, Peg.

PEG moves away to serve the other MAN. LLOYD continues in quieter tones.

LLOYD: Yes. I knew her. Not very well though.

MIKE: How well?

LLOYD: (*After a glance, to see if anyone is standing near him*) One night only, old boy. Then a chum whispered in my ear, and you couldn't see my heels for dust.

MIKE has taken a sudden dislike to LLOYD, but he tries not to show it.

MIKE: When was this?

LLOYD: Oh, six or seven months ago. Perhaps longer.

MIKE: And what exactly did this chum of yours …

LLOYD: Said she wasn't above a spot of blackmail. That was enough for me. I don't mind paying for my pleasure – have to – but there's a limit.

MIKE: You came to the party that night …

LLOYD smiles a little foolishly and holds up his drink.

LLOYD: My trouble, old boy. I was full to the scalp that night. Ingrid, that Swedish kid I was with, picked me up. Said she wanted to take me to a party. As soon as I realised it was at the old "Hotbed" … (*He shakes his head*) I was out of there as fast as my little rubber legs could carry me.

MIKE: And what about Bob West? How does he fit into all this?

LLOYD: Bob West? Who's Bob West?

MIKE: The chap behind the bar – the landlord?

LLOYD: Oh, I know the character you mean. (*Shaking his head*) Don't know anything about him, old man.

MIKE: Sel told me he was her uncle.

LLOYD: Well, perhaps he is. But if you ask me, I think all those kids are told what to say, and what not to say. And if they put a foot wrong … (*He draws his finger across his throat*) I've been around quite a bit, but I'm not rugged enough to get mixed up in that kind of set-up.

MIKE: You mean – you think there was someone 'behind' Sel …?

LLOYD: Why, yes – don't you? Sel, Ingrid, all those kids. Someone's running them all right, I'm sure of it. (*Cautiously; making sure that he is not overheard*) Why, look what happened to that other youngster … What was her name? Della something or other …

MIKE: (*Puzzled*) I don't know who you mean?

LLOYD: It was in the paper, old boy – if you remember. She used to hang around the old "Hotbed", was one of the regulars. Then she broke away and instead of keeping her mouth shut …

MIKE: (*Suddenly*) Oh, I remember! … A chorus girl … Notting Hill Gate. She was stabbed.

LLOYD: That's right … Notting Hill Gate … You've got it. (*Shaking his head*) Damn funny business that … Damn funny business altogether …

MIKE: (*Surprised*) But was she a friend of Sel's?

LLOYD: Oh, I don't know about that. (*Thoughtfully*) Yes, come to think of it, I suppose she must have been. (*Taking hold of MIKE's arm*) But look here, old man, you take my tip and don't dig too deep into all this, or you'll finish up with a knife in your back.

LLOYD gulps down his drink. NIGEL returns and joins them.

55

NIGEL: Ready?

LLOYD: (*Breezily*) Yes, we're ready, Nigel. Now – let's take a look at this old heap you're passing off on me.

CUT TO: Tall Trees. Belford-on-Thames. Night. Later the same night.

NIGEL's car, the M.G., pulls into the drive and stops. MIKE gets out, waves good night to NIGEL, and goes to the front door. NIGEL's car moves off down the drive. MIKE lets himself into the house.

CUT TO: Tall Trees. The Hall. Night.

MIKE closes the front door behind him. He looks tired and dejected. He hangs up his coat and hat and moves to the drawing room door.

CUT TO: Tall Trees. The Drawing Room. Night.

MIKE enters and stands transfixed, staring in the direction of the fireplace. RUTH HILTON is standing, waiting for MIKE.

RUTH: Hello, Mike …

MIKE remains at the door, speechless for a moment; then he goes to RUTH, not knowing quite what to say.

MIKE: I thought you were in Paris …?

RUTH: I was this afternoon …

MIKE hesitates, then, deeply moved, half turns towards the drinks table.

MIKE: You must be tired. Let me get you a drink.

RUTH: No, I don't want a drink.

There is a pause.

MIKE: Why did you come back, Ruth?

RUTH: Don't you know why? What did you expect me to do when you're in trouble like this?

56

MIKE turns sharply to look at RUTH. Her expression is sympathetic, appealing. He goes slowly to her then quickly takes her in his arms.

CUT TO: Tall Trees. The Terrace of the Sun Parlour.
MIKE stands, smoking as he talks, looking out across the garden into the darkness. RUTH is seated listening as MIKE comes to the end of his story.

MIKE: … I didn't tell the police I intended to stay the weekend on the houseboat. (*He glances quickly at RUTH*) In any case, I'd changed my mind on the way down there.

RUTH: So, your alibi really depends on finding this boy?

MIKE: Yes.

RUTH: Well, surely, he must be a local boy, if he was on the common on his own.

MIKE: <u>If</u> he was on the common.

RUTH stares at MIKE uncomprehendingly. MIKE stubs his cigarette with an angry gesture.

RUTH: What do you mean?

MIKE: O'Day doesn't believe the boy exists. Perhaps he's right. Perhaps I dreamed the whole thing up.

RUTH: Darling, don't be absurd!

MIKE: Well, the police can't find him, Ruth.

RUTH rises, looking at MIKE with a determined expression.

RUTH: Then we will!

CUT TO: The Common. Day.
MIKE is sitting in the driving seat of his car. He is watching as RUTH is questioning a group of children some thirty yards away on the common. She leaves them and returns to the car. The children continue playing with a ball. RUTH shakes her head as she approaches the car.

57

CUT TO: A Cinema in Belford. Day.

A noisy queue of children are waiting for the door to open to admit them to a Saturday morning matinée. MIKE's car drives slowly past.

As it drives past the queue MIKE scans the faces of the children; RUTH watches him anxiously. They reach the end of the queue. MIKE looks at RUTH despairingly and drives on. RUTH looks worried.

CUT TO: A Road near a River. Day.

MIKE's car is approaching in the distance. On the riverbank, about thirty yards away, a BOY is crouched, back to camera, engrossed in something on the ground. The car approaches the bend in the foreground and is turning off in the opposite direction to the boy, when the BOY suddenly jumps to his feet. He is holding a sailing boat and bears a strong resemblance, both in dress and appearance, to the boy MIKE is looking for.

CUT TO: MIKE's Car. Day.

RUTH sees the boy.

RUTH: Mike! Look!

MIKE stops the car and looks towards the BOY.

MIKE: My God, it is!

MIKE jumps out of the car. RUTH watches his progress excitedly as she gets out of the car.

CUT TO: The Riverbank. Day.

MIKE runs towards the boy, who still has his back to the camera. He is adjusting the sails of his toy yacht. RUTH has got out of the car and she, too, is moving towards the boy. MIKE is only a few yards from the river when the BOY turns to put the boat into the water. MIKE stops dead. The BOY stares at Mike in obvious surprise, never having seen him before.

CUT TO: A Small Country Fair. Night.

This is one of those small travelling fairs that stay three or four nights in a village and move on. MIKE's car is parked on the grass verge near the entrance.

CUT TO: The Helter-Skelter. Night.

The tense, thrilled, excited face of a ten-year-old BOY as he wizzes on the mat to the camera which pans with him as he goes past, to reveal MIKE and RUTH standing nearby watching the children as they come down the ride. MIKE looks wearily at the next boy as he reaches the alighting point. He smiles faintly and fumbles for his matches.

CUT TO: The Dodgem Car Ride. Night.

A mad hurly-burly of dodgem cars. There are BOYS in several of the cars. There are wild cries and blaring music.

MIKE, standing on the side, scans the faces in the cars, wearily, hopelessly. The cries of the children seem to be mocking him. He passes his hand across his forehead with a swift, frantic gesture. RUTH looks concerned. She takes MIKE's arm.

RUTH: I think we'd better call it a day.

MIKE looks at RUTH vaguely.

MIKE: Yes … Yes, I suppose so.

MIKE and RUTH move away.

CUT TO: The Drive of Tall Trees. Night.

MIKE's car turns into the drive and stops several yards from the garage. One door of the garage is open, the other having blown closed. RUTH gets out of the car and opens the garage door. MIKE turns on his headlights and the car starts to move forward.

CUT TO: The Garage at Tall Trees. Night.

MIKE's car drives into the garage and stops. MIKE stares into the camera. Something on the wall has riveted his attention. He switches off the engine and calls RUTH as he gets out of the car. RUTH joins him.

RUTH: What is it …?

RUTH's voice trails away as she follows MIKE's gaze. The camera pans to show the rear wall; a tyre hangs on a hook. Suspended from this hook is – THE KITE.

MIKE and RUTH exchange bewildered glances and MIKE goes quickly to the kite, taking it down from the hook. He examines it and RUTH joins him. RUTH looks at the kite in MIKE's hands.

RUTH: Someone has a weird sense of humour.

MIKE shakes his head slowly.

MIKE: It's the same kite …

RUTH stares at MIKE dumbfoundedly. MIKE looks at RUTH.

MIKE: It's the same one, Ruth!

CUT TO: Tall Trees. The Hall. Night.

The telephone is heard ringing in the drawing room as MIKE and RUTH come in at the front door. RUTH is carrying the kite. MIKE glances at RUTH, then moves quickly to the drawing room door.

CUT TO: Tall Trees. The Drawing Room. Night.

The telephone is still ringing. MIKE enters and crosses to the receiver, taking it up.

MIKE: (*On the phone*) Hello …?

There is the sound of someone pressing Button 'A' in a call box, coins dropping, and then a faintly muffled MAN's VOICE comes on the line.

VOICE: (*On the other end of the phone*) Mike Hilton?

MIKE: Yes – who is that?

VOICE: You found the kite?

MIKE hesitates, glancing at RUTH as she comes into the room. She sees his expression and goes to him, laying the kite down on the settee as she passes it.

MIKE: (*Tensely*) Yes, I found it.

VOICE: Now you'd like to find the boy, wouldn't you?

MIKE is speechless for a moment. He looks bewilderedly at RUTH.

VOICE: Well, Mr Hilton, d'you want to know where the boy is, or don't you?

MIKE: (*A note of desperation in his voice*) Yes, of course I want to know!

VOICE: (*Quietly; after a tiny pause*) Then meet me tomorrow morning.

MIKE: … But who is that? Who is it speaking?

VOICE: I'll see you tomorrow morning; eleven o'clock – and don't mention this to anyone, because if you do …

MIKE: (*Quickly*) I shan't mention it to anyone – but who are you? Where are you speaking from?

VOICE: Do you know Dubinsky's bookshop?

MIKE: (*Puzzled*) Dubinsky's bookshop? … No …

VOICE: It's in Chelsea – on the King's Road – about two hundred yards from The Fourposter. I'll see you there tomorrow morning … Eleven o'clock …

MIKE: (*Hesitantly*) Yes … Yes, all right … (*Suddenly*) But look here, hadn't you better tell me who you are, otherwise I shan't …

There is the sound of a click as the receiver is replaced at the other end. MIKE looks at RUTH as he replaces his own receiver. RUTH has obviously got the gist of the conversation.

RUTH: (*Tensely*) He knows where the boy is?

MIKE: Yes …

RUTH: Who was it, Mike?

MIKE: (*Thoughtfully*) I don't know.

CUT TO: Outside DUBINSKY's Bookshop. King's Road. Chelsea. Day.

The shop windows and troughs outside still contain mostly second-hand books, but there are now some new books, mostly paperbacks, in racks at the entrance to the shop. A GIRL stands in the entrance studying the titles in these racks.

CUT TO: Inside DUBINSKY's Bookshop. Day.

Floor to ceiling, bookshelves cover the walls. A door, partly open, leads to another room at the rear of the shop. Another large independent bookshelf lies parallel to the rear wall, and it is in this alley of books that CHRIS BENSON stands on a small pair of steps, dusting the books. He peers anxiously through a gap in the books towards the entrance, then glances in DUBINSKY's direction.

DUBINSKY sits at a small table near the cash desk, cutting cartridge paper into strips with a large pair of scissors. The GIRL we saw in the entrance approaches with a book she has selected.

GIRL: I'll take this one.

DUBINSKY: Three-and-six, please.

CHRIS watches DUBINSKY serve the girl, then he comes down the steps and goes to the table. DUBINSKY gives the girl her book and change.

GIRL: Thank you. Good morning.

DUBINSKY: Good morning. Come again, please.

The GIRL goes.

CHRIS: You get off if you like, Louis. I can manage all right.

DUBINSKY: I'll wait till you've been out for lunch. You know these hospitals. I may not be back for hours.

CHRIS: Makes no difference to me. I've got sandwiches anyway.

62

DUBINSKY: Well, in that case …

DUBINSKY takes up his jacket from the back of the chair and puts it on.

DUBINSKY: If it's nothing serious, I shouldn't be too long.

CHRIS: It's nothing serious, Louis – now don't worry.

DUBINSKY: I hope not. Here – some cigarettes.

CHRIS makes to protest but DUBINSKY shoves them into his hands.

DUBINSKY: I see you only had one left. It will save you going out.

CHRIS nods his thanks. DUBINSKY goes out. CHRIS looks at his watch, then lights a cigarette from the packet DUBINSKY gave him. He looks thoughtful, tapping the packet on the table in an agitated manner. With an impatient gesture he takes up the scissors and carries on DUBINSKY's task of cutting up the cartridge paper. CHRIS looks up.

RUBY STEVENSON is standing in the doorway looking at CHRIS. She hurries towards him, opening her handbag.

RUBY: I thought he was never going. Here we are, Chris.

RUBY takes an envelope from her handbag and gives it to CHRIS. He doesn't take it; he just looks at it. RUBY's face hardens momentarily.

RUBY: For heaven's sake, Chris! You don't want to go on like this, do you? Doing part-time jobs for peanuts?

CHRIS relents, taking the envelope from her. But he is still uncertain. RUBY takes a cigarette from CHRIS's packet on the table. She holds it up to her mouth and CHRIS lights it from the end of his own cigarette. RUBY looks at him as he does this, glancing down to indicate the envelope.

RUBY: You understand – he mustn't get hold of this. Just let him take a look.

63

RUBY sees CHRIS's hand as he holds the cigarette; it is trembling.

CHRIS: And what if he won't play?

RUBY: He'll play all right. Wouldn't you, if you were in his shoes?

CHRIS nods vaguely. RUBY takes his hand in hers, squeezing it as if to impart strength to him.

RUBY: Don't worry, Chris. Everything's going to be all right. This time tomorrow we'll be in Paris.

RUBY kisses CHRIS lingeringly on the cheek. He is still unsure.

CHRIS: What do I do when I've seen him?

RUBY: Go back to my flat and wait. I'll phone you.

CHRIS nods.

CUT TO: Outside DUBINSKY's Bookshop. King's Road. Chelsea. Day.

About twenty yards down the street MIKE's car has drawn into the kerb and MIKE is getting out. He walks down to the bookshop window and lingers there for a moment, trying to peer through the books into the interior of the shop. He can see nothing of interest. He goes into the shop.

CUT TO: DUBINSKY's Bookshop. Day.

A prospective CUSTOMER scans the bookshop – an introspective face, watery eyes peering at titles through thick lenses. As he turns away from a shelf, he sees MIKE staring at him. MIKE looks quickly away. The MAN gives him an odd look and hurries out. MIKE glances after him.

CHRIS: Good morning, Mr Hilton.

MIKE turns to see CHRIS standing in the open doorway at the rear of the shop. CHRIS laughs a little nervously, as MIKE stares at him. He talks rapidly as he goes to the front, reversing the "open" sign to "closed". He is obviously terrified of the prospect of this interview and is covering this with an offhand manner, overdone to the point of being downright insolent.

CHRIS: You didn't recognise my voice on the phone, did you? Didn't think you would. Always been a pretty good mimic … Don't know why the devil I didn't take it up – professionally, I mean. There's a lot of money in it, you know, especially if …

MIKE: (*Cutting in*) If you don't mind, I'm in rather a hurry. Get to the point.

CHRIS is now standing with his back to the shop door. He breaks away nervously under MIKE's gaze and moves to the table, his fingers running agitatedly along a bookshelf as he goes.

CHRIS: I've got a friend who wants to go abroad, and … (*He hesitates*)

MIKE: Go on …

CHRIS: This friend of mine knows where the boy is – the boy you're looking for.

MIKE: Get to the point. How much?

CHRIS: Well – (*He hesitates*) My friend's figure is – six thousand pounds.

MIKE: (*Impassively*) Six thousand?

CHRIS: Yes …

MIKE appears to be considering the proposition.

MIKE: And what proof have I got that your friend is telling the truth?

CHRIS: The kite …

MIKE: (*Shaking his head*) Before I part with six thousand pounds, I want a great deal more proof than that.

CHRIS looks at MIKE for a moment, then moves a little away, taking the envelope from his pocket as he does so.

CHRIS: All right – what about this?

CHRIS takes a photograph out of the envelope and holds it up for MIKE to see. It is an enlarged snapshot of the boy MIKE met on the day of the murder.

MIKE stares at the photograph in silence for a moment. CHRIS smiles as he slowly returns the photograph to the envelope. He is beginning to feel a little more confident now. The interview is not quite so terrifying as he thought it would be.

CHRIS: Well? What do I tell my friend?

CHRIS looks at MIKE, awaiting his reply, fully expecting his complete co-operation.

MIKE: You can tell him this. If he's depending on me for a trip abroad, he'd better resign himself to 'holidays at home'.

CHRIS's face falls. The nervousness has gone now. It is replaced by a spark of anger.

CHRIS: You'd better think again. Believe me, without my friend's help you haven't a dog's chance of finding that boy …

MIKE: "Hadn't" a dog's chance.

CHRIS stares at MIKE bewilderedly.

MIKE: We had nothing to go on. Now things are different.

MIKE glances down at the envelope in CHRIS's hands. CHRIS realises MIKE's intention. He backs away colliding with a corner of the desk. Paper and drawing pins fall to the floor. MIKE moves menacingly towards him. CHRIS continues to back away.

CHRIS: All right! If you're not going to fork out, that's that. Get out of here!

MIKE: Not without that photograph.

They 'cat and mouse' on opposite sides of the table, CHRIS hastily stuffing the envelope back into his pocket.

CHRIS, sensing MIKE's determination, is thoroughly frightened now. MIKE moves around the table towards him.

DUBINSKY:	And you think they'll believe your story – about Chris and the photograph?
MIKE:	(*Exasperated*) They've got to believe it!
DUBINSKY:	(*Shaking his head*) But they won't – you know that as well as I do. (*Quietly; taking the empty glass out of MIKE's hand*) Mr Hilton, I've known Chris a long time. There's no real harm in the boy. I'd hate to see him get into trouble.
MIKE:	(*Irritatedly; still feeling his jaw*) Well – what do you suggest?
DUBINSKY:	You want that photograph, don't you?

MIKE nods.

DUBINSKY:	Then let me talk to Chris – let me try and get it for you.

MIKE looks at DUBINSKY; then hesitates. DUBINSKY surveys the chaos created by the fight.

DUBINSKY:	After all, my friend, I think you owe me a favour. Don't you agree?
MIKE:	(*Nodding; the ghost of a smile*) Yes, I do. I'm sorry, Dubinsky; (*He indicates the room*) but don't worry, I'll pay for all this.
DUBINSKY:	No, no, that's not important – just let me have a word with Chris first, before you go to the police.

MIKE hesitates again, then nods.

MIKE:	All right – we'll try it your way.

CUT TO: A Street in Fulham. Day.

This is a street of dilapidated houses in the poorer part of Fulham; terraced houses with steps to the front door and basement flats.

MIKE's car appears, and pulls in to the kerb. DUBINSKY gets out of the car, nods to MIKE, and then hurries along the pavement. He turns into one of the houses and goes down the basement steps.

He knocks at the door. After a few moments he goes to the window and peers in.

WOMAN's VOICE: (*Off screen*) The door's always open.

DUBINSKY starts, looking up. The WOMAN is seated on the balustrade above, near the front door, nursing a baby and smoking a cigarette.

DUBINSKY: Oh – er – thanks.

DUBINSKY goes to the door, smiles uneasily at the WOMAN who is still staring at him, opens the door and goes in.

CUT TO: CHRIS BENSON's Studio-Living Room. Fulham. Day.

DUBINSKY closes the door and stands there looking around the room. There are paintings stacked on an old settee; a half empty bottle of milk on the table alongside of a pot of brushes and a jar of jam with a knife stuck in it. A half-completed canvas is on an easel. There is no lampshade, just the naked bulb hanging from the ceiling for maximum light. Some old frames are stacked near a partly open door. DUBINSKY crosses to this door.

DUBINSKY: Chris!

CUT TO: The Adjoining Room. Day.

DUBINSKY looks into the room, which is CHRIS's bedroom. An unmade, grubby-sheeted bed is in the foreground. There is no sign of Chris. DUBINSKY frowns and goes out.

CUT TO: CHRIS BENSON's Studio-Living Room. Fulham. Day.

DUBINSKY hurries to the door. He hesitates as something at floor-level catches his eye. He crouches, uncovering a painting partly obscured by another. He looks at the painting. It is a

70

partly finished portrait of RUBY STEVENSON. There are footsteps on the basement steps. DUBINSKY looks sharply towards the door. He rises as the steps outside approach the door.

MRS POOLE enters. She is about forty-five, with curlers under a headscarf, eyes screwed up to avoid the smoke from her cigarette.

MRS POOLE: Oh, 'ullo. It's only you then. Myrtle said there was a visitor.

DUBINSKY: Mrs Poole – I'm looking for Chris. Has he been here since he left this morning?

MRS POOLE chuckles.

MRS POOLE: This morning? 'E left 'ere Monday.

DUBINSKY: Monday? That's three days ago.

MRS POOLE nods.

DUBINSKY: Well, where is he? Where's he staying?

MRS POOLE shrugs. Her eyes stray to the unfinished portrait of RUBY STEVENSON.

DUBINSKY: Is he staying with Miss Stevenson?

MRS POOLE: Don't ask me.

DUBINSKY glances down at the painting.

DUBINSKY: Where does she live – do you know?

MRS POOLE: She did live in Coster Street, but she's just moved. Always on the move if you ask me.

DUBINSKY: Well – where has she moved to?

MRS POOLE: Somewhere posh. I think it's Stratford Mansions. (*A shrug*) Don't know what the 'ell Chris sees in her. She's old enough to be 'is mum.

DUBINSKY: Thank you, Mrs Poole.

DUBINSKY bows politely and goes out. MRS POOLE stares after him, then looks at the painting again, jealously mimicking the haughty expression of the subject.

CUT TO: Stratford Mansions. Chelsea. Day.

This is a five-storey block of flats, not luxury, but infinitely superior to CHRIS BENSON's establishment.

MIKE's car drives up and MIKE and DUBINSKY get out.

CUT TO: The Hall of Stratford Mansions. Chelsea. Day.

There is a lift and stairs.

A five-year-old GIRL playing with a ball; throwing it up the stairs and watching it dribble down before catching it. MIKE and DUBINSKY enter. MIKE looks at the notice board. DUBINSKY smiles at the little girl who stops playing at them.

MIKE: Her name isn't on the board …

DUBINSKY: No? …

MIKE: Of course, if she's just moved in, it probably wouldn't be.

DUBINSKY has an idea. He crouches down, talking to the little girl.

DUBINSKY: Do you know a lady called Miss Stevenson?

MIKE smiles faintly to himself. After all, the girl is only five. She looks blankly at DUBINSKY.

GIRL: I've got a new ball.

DUBINSKY: (*Wryly*) That's nice, isn't it?

MIKE: Well – we'd better start at the first floor and work our way up.

MIKE rings for the lift. DUBINSKY rises and looks at the notice board.

GIRL: The new lady bought it for me.

It is a second or two before MIKE and DUBINSKY realise the significance of the little girl's words. They look at one another. MIKE turns to the little girl.

MIKE: The new lady, eh? And – er – where does the new lady live? Which floor?

GIRL: Right up the top. A two and a one!

MIKE tousles the GIRL's hair. DUBINSKY takes out a two-shilling piece and gives it to the girl.

DUBINSKY: There. When that ball's worn out you buy another one, eh?

MIKE and DUBINSKY get into the lift. The GIRL beams at the money in her hand, then, immediately dismissing the incident from her mind, begins throwing the ball up the stairs again.

CUT TO: Stratford Mansions. 5th Floor. Landing. Day.

The number 21 is clearly marked on the door right opposite the lift.

The lift arrives and MIKE and DUBINSKY get out. MIKE crosses to the door to ring the bell, then hesitates. He glances at DUBINSKY. Music is heard faintly from inside the flat. DUBINSKY nods, he too has heard the music. MIKE rings the bell. After a moment the music stops. DUBINSKY and MIKE exchange meaning glances. MIKE rings the bell again. Silence. MIKE has an idea. He puts a hand to his lips and indicates the lift, motioning to DUBINSKY to take it down. DUBINSKY winks understandingly, opens the lift gates noisily, gets in, closes the gates and descends. MIKE remains there a moment watching the lift go down. He crouches in preparation for a look through the keyhole. There is a noise within the flat. In a flash MIKE flattens himself against the adjacent wall, his eyes fixed on the door. Silence. The door handle turns, and the door is cautiously opened. MIKE springs forward, jamming his foot in the opening. The door is slammed against it. With a tremendous heave, MIKE barges into the hall.

CUT TO: RUBY STEVENSON's Flat. Day.

MIKE hurtles into the hall, half falling to the floor. The other MAN has been flung aside and is partly hidden by the open door. He runs out of the flat as MIKE turns to grasp him, slamming the door behind him. MIKE swears under his breath and wrenches the door open.

CUT TO: Stratford Mansions. 5th Floor. Landing. Day.
MIKE runs out of the flat. The echoing sound of the MAN's footsteps is heard as he runs down the stairs. MIKE dashes to the lift, then, realising he hasn't got time to wait for it, he runs down the stairs in pursuit.

CUT TO: Stratford Mansions. 4th Floor Landing. Day.
The MAN is just disappearing down the stairs leading to the third floor. MIKE is racing down to the fourth floor.

CUT TO: Stratford Mansions. 3rd Floor Landing. Day.
The MAN flashes past the grills of the lift-shaft. MIKE turns onto the stairs from the fourth floor landing, runs down several stairs, then leaps down over the remainder onto the third floor landing.

CUT TO: Stratford Mansions. 2nd Floor Landing. Day.
MIKE has obviously gained ground with his leap.

CUT TO: Stratford Mansions. 1st Floor Landing. Day.
The MAN skids across the landing and starts to run down these stairs. MIKE is close on his heels when he suddenly collides with an OLD LADY approaching the stairs. He is forced to stop for a vital few seconds to apologise.

CUT TO: Stratford Mansions. The Hall and Stairs. Day.
The MAN races downstairs to the ground floor. We now see that he is CHRIS BENSON. The GIRL who was previously playing with the ball has flattened herself against the wall, looking fearfully up at him. CHRIS doesn't notice the girl's ball on the stair. He steps on it and slips, falling, rolling down the remainder of the stairs. MIKE runs down looking down at CHRIS. DUBINSKY runs towards CHRIS from the direction of the lift. MIKE hurries down the stairs.

74

CHRIS is on the floor, with both hands clasped over his right ankle, an expression of agony on his face. The GIRL stares blankly on as DUBINSKY crouches, concerned over CHRIS's ankle. MIKE runs down the remainder of the stairs and looks breathlessly at CHRIS.

CUT TO: The Living Room of RUBY STEVENSON's Flat.
The flat is furnished mainly with moderately priced modern furniture. On the walls are framed photographs of variety artists, old friends of RUBY STEVENSON's.

CHRIS is sitting on the settee, still clutching his ankle. DUBINSKY stands nearby holding a glass of water and a couple of aspirin. CHRIS accepts these grudgingly as MIKE walks over to him. MIKE holds a photograph – the one of the boy that CHRIS showed him in the bookshop. CHRIS's attitude to MIKE is stubborn. To DUBINSKY, he shows the anger and resentment of being "shopped" by a friend.

MIKE: … you still haven't told me the boy's name.

CHRIS: I don't know his name!

MIKE: I don't believe you!

CHRIS: All right, you don't believe me!

DUBINSKY: Chris, don't be stupid, there's a good chap – we're only trying to help you.

CHRIS: (*With sarcasm*) Oh, sure – sure – you're very anxious to help me, aren't you, Dubinsky?

MIKE: (*Losing his temper*) If he isn't why the hell d'you think he's here? But believe me, I'm not so anxious. I don't care two hoots what happens to you. All I want …

CHRIS: Is to save your skin, I know.

MIKE loses control completely at this and grabs CHRIS by the lapels.

MIKE: You listen to me! You're going to tell me all I …

CHRIS cries out in agony as he is twisted around on his ankle. DUBINSKY lays a restraining arm on MIKE, then looks hard at CHRIS.

DUBINSKY: Well – what is it you want to know?

MIKE: (*Holding up the photograph*) Who is this boy?

CHRIS: I've told you, I don't know. Ruby calls him, "Pal", but that's just his nickname. I don't know who he is. (*He looks at DUBINSKY*) That's the truth, Louis. I swear it.

DUBINSKY: (*Gently*) All right, Chris. I believe you. Now tell us what happened between you and Ruby?

CHRIS: It was last Sunday might; she asked me to call round and see her. When I arrived she was het-up, excited.

DUBINSKY: Go on …

CHRIS: She started to talk about Selby – about the murder. She said she knew who did it and if we played our cards carefully there was a heap of money in it for us.

MIKE stares at CHRIS.

MIKE: Did she give you any idea who it was?

CHRIS: No. But I'm almost sure it's the man she works for. He runs a call-girl racket. She's never mentioned his name.

DUBINSKY: Did she tell you anything else?

CHRIS: She showed me the kite and the photograph.

MIKE: Did she say where she got them from?

CHRIS: No, but it's obvious, isn't it? She stole them from the boy's father.

MIKE: The boy's father? But how would Ruby get to know …

MIKE stops suddenly as the truth dawns on him. DUBINSKY is completely bewildered. He looks at MIKE.

MIKE: (*To DUBINSKY*) Don't you see? The boy's
                 father, and the man Ruby works for, are one
                 and the same person! (*Snapping his fingers*)
                 That's why we haven't found the boy! If he
                 committed the murder, then naturally Pal – or
                 whatever his name is – would be kept under
                 lock and key.

MIKE's thoughts are racing now, he looks quickly at CHRIS.

MIKE: This man – Ruby's boss – have you any idea
                 where he lives?

CHRIS shakes his head.

CHRIS: She's always been very cagey about him. All I
                 know is, she makes trips into the country to
                 visit her "sister".

MIKE: Where? What part of the country?

CHRIS: I don't know. I've never been interested. She
                 takes a Green Line Coach, that's all I know.

DUBINSKY: Is she with her "sister" now?

CHRIS: I don't know where she is. (*To MIKE*) She told
                 me to come back here after I'd seen you and
                 wait until …

CHRIS is interrupted by the telephone ringing in the next room.
MIKE and DUBINSKY look towards the bedroom.

CHRIS: That's probably Ruby – she said she'd phone.

MIKE: All right. Answer it.

CHRIS: (*Tensely*) That's all very well, but what the hell
                 do I say?

MIKE hesitates.

MIKE: Tell her you've seen me, and I've agreed to pay
                 the money. Say you'll wait for her here.

*CHRIS isn't sure whether he wants to do this or not. He looks
at DUBINSKY who gives a friendly little nod of
encouragement.*

DUBINSKY: Go on, Chris.

77

DUBINSKY helps CHRIS to his feet. As the phone continues ringing, CHRIS crosses to the bedroom door and opens it. He stops dead, staring into the room. The others look at him curiously.

CUT TO: RUBY STEVENSON's Flat. The Bedroom. Day.
CHRIS enters and stares in the direction of the bed. DUBINSKY and MIKE appear behind him. CHRIS stares around the bedroom. There is chaos. Clothes have been torn from the wardrobe and chest of drawers. The lamp has been swept from the bedside table onto the floor. The body of a woman lies half on, half off the bed. Her eyes stare sightlessly up at the ceiling. A nylon stocking hangs limply from her throat. It is RUBY STEVENSON. The telephone continues to ring.

CUT TO: The Living Room of RUBY STEVENSON's Flat. Day. About an hour later.
CHRIS is seated, his right leg hanging over the arm of the chair; he regards his painful ankle from time to time. DUBINSKY is seated on the other arm of the chair. Through the partly open bedroom door we can see a Fingerprint Expert and various other police experts at work near the bed. MIKE stands looking at SUPERINTENDENT O'DAY who is casually studying the photograph of the boy.

O'DAY: … (*To CHRIS*) You say she called him Pal?

CHRIS: Yes, but it was just a nickname. I doubt whether anyone else calls him that.

O'DAY: I imagine they must do, or she wouldn't have used the name. Anyway, it's something to go on – something definite for a change.

O'DAY looks at the photograph again.

MIKE: That's obviously what he was after – the photograph.

78

O'DAY: (*Not looking up*) I agree, Mr Hilton.

MIKE: He found out she was double-crossing him and
             …

O'DAY: (*Still not looking up; interrupting MIKE*) I
             agree, Mr Hilton.

MIKE: (*Irritated*) Well, if you agree, it's a pity you
             don't do something about it!

O'DAY looks up at MIKE.

O'DAY: What would you suggest, sir?

MIKE: I suggest you find out who the man is!

O'DAY: (*Unperturbed*) But we've been trying to find
             out, sir. We've been trying ever since your
             friend Miss Brooks was murdered.

DUBINSKY: (*Quietly*) So you think the man who murdered
             Selby also … (*He nods towards the bedroom*)

O'DAY looks at DUBINSKY and gives a little nod.

O'DAY: Yes, I do. I do, Mr Dubinsky.

*CRADDOCK comes out of the bedroom; he is carrying an
address book belonging to RUBY STEVENSON.*

CRADDOCK: (*Handing O'DAY the book*) We found this in a
             drawer by the bed. It's her address book.

*O'DAY takes the book, opens it, and carefully studies the
names and addresses.*

O'DAY: (*To CRADDOCK*) What's this Rickmansworth
             number – there's no name with it?

CRADDOCK: I don't know. The Sergeant's checking it.

*O'DAY nods and continues to examine the book. MIKE watches
him, is about to speak, then hesitates. O'DAY senses that MIKE
wants to ask him something.*

O'DAY: (*After a moment; quietly*) Well, Mr Hilton –
             what is it?

MIKE: O'Day, there's something I want to know –
             something I've got to know in fact.

O'DAY: (*Looking up*) Go ahead. If I can help you, I
                will.

MIKE: Well, the first time we met you said that
                Selby Brooks was … (*He hesitates*)

O'DAY: I told you she was a notorious character.

MIKE: Yes.

O'DAY gives a little nod.

O'DAY: I was telling you the truth, Mr Hilton. I
                wasn't just talking for effect, using shock
                tactics, if that's what you're thinking. She
                was a professional blackmailer. It's my
                guess that's why she was   murdered.

MIKE: (*Almost aggressively*) Well, all I can say is –
                she didn't blackmail me!

O'DAY: (*Quite sincere; no suggestion of cynicism*)
                No? Well, perhaps she didn't want to.
                Perhaps she was in love with you, Mr
                Hilton. All kinds of people fall in love.

MIKE: But that's not what you think?

O'DAY: No, that's not what I think. I think she was
                preparing the ground. She knew you were
                pretty well off and ultimately, in my
                opinion, she'd have told you she was
                pregnant, and she'd have   blackmailed you.
                That was the usual form, Mr   Hilton.

MIKE: (*Shaking his head*) I – I – just don't believe
                that.

O'DAY: Well, I could be wrong of course. I could be
                very wrong. (*He hands MIKE the address
                book*) There's a whole list of names and
                phone numbers in here. I want you to tell
                me if any of these people were at that party
                you went to.

MIKE takes the book and opens it.

MIKE:	(*After a pause*) … I remember some of these names … (*Reading*) Ingrid … Vida … Iris … Chris … (*He looks across at CHRIS*) Bob West … Louis Dubinsky … (*He glances at DUBINSKY*) … I don't seem to know any of the others.
O'DAY:	There's a phone number on the back page …
MIKE:	(*Looking at the book*) Rickmansworth 0734?
O'DAY:	That's right. Have you any idea who it belongs to?
MIKE:	No, I'm afraid I haven't. (*Handing back the book to O'DAY*) But why did you ask me about the party?
CRADDOCK:	We think the murderer was at that party and that's how he got hold of the newspaper. The one we found on the houseboat.
MIKE:	(*Thoughtfully*) Yes, that's possible, I suppose. Immediately I did the trick Sel and I went out to get a breath of fresh air.

DETECTIVE SERGEANT BELLAMY comes out of the bedroom; he carries a sheet of notepaper in his hand.

BELLAMY:	Excuse me, sir.
O'DAY:	Yes, Sergeant?
BELLAMY:	We've checked the Rickmansworth number. It's a private subscriber, sir – he's not in the book. (*He looks at the notepaper*) P.A. Lloyd, Longacre Farm, Welton Cross.
MIKE:	(*Surprised*) Lloyd?

CHRIS looks up. He, too, recognises the name.

O'DAY:	Do you know anyone called Lloyd?
MIKE:	Yes, I do. Peter Lloyd – he's a car salesman. (*To CRADDOCK*) He's a friend of Nigel Green's. (*Suddenly; to O'DAY*) He was at that

	party, he turned up with one of the girls I mentioned – Ingrid.
BELLAMY:	Ingrid? (*To MIKE; curious*) A tall, good looking blonde – Swedish?
MIKE:	Yes.

BELLAMY looks across at O'DAY and gives a brief nod, obviously signifying "Yes, she's one of them". The INSPECTOR notices this and quickly turns towards MIKE.

| CRADDOCK: | Was this man a friend of Selby's? |
| MIKE: | No, but he'd met her. As a matter of fact, I've seen Lloyd quite recently. (*Puzzled*) If this is the same chap, I'm surprised he lives out at Welton Cross because he spends an awful lot of time in the West … |

MIKE stops; a sudden thought has occurred to him. He moves towards BELLAMY.

MIKE:	What did you say his initials were?
BELLAMY:	(*Looking at the notepaper*) P.A. …
MIKE:	P.A. Lloyd?
BELLAMY:	(*Puzzled*) Yes.

MIKE suddenly takes the sheet of paper from BELLAMY and stares at it.

O'DAY:	(*Irritated*) What are you getting at?
MIKE:	I'm wondering if Lloyd's got a boy with the same initials, because if he has … (*He taps the notepaper*) P … A … L …
CRADDOCK	*and O'DAY look at one another.*
CRADDOCK:	Of course!
O'DAY:	(*Under his breath*) Pal …

CUT TO: A Country Lane near Welton Cross. Day.
A police car bumps to a halt at a gap in a fence. A weather-beaten notice board is nailed to the end post; the words

"Longacre Farm" are barely discernible. The car turns into the gap and starts down the drive to the house.

CUT TO: Longacre Farm. Day.
This is a faintly dilapidated three-storeyed house in several acres of ground. The land is wild and long grass borders the drive leading to the house.
The police car stops outside the house and CRADDOCK and O'DAY move to the front door. CRADDOCK is carrying a large envelope.
At the front door O'DAY presses the bellpush. CRADDOCK looks around with obvious interest.

CRADDOCK: Pity it's been let go. Sort of place I've always wanted.
O'DAY: (*Drily*) You can have it! I wouldn't like to tackle that grass on a Sunday morning.

O'DAY tries the knocker. They hear footsteps inside the hall and a moment later the door is opened. PETER LLOYD stands there.

O'DAY: Good morning, sir. Mr Peter Lloyd?
LLOYD: That's right …
O'DAY: We're police officers, sir. We think you might be able to help us in some enquiries we're making.
LLOYD: I see. Well – won't you come in?
O'DAY: Thank you, sir.

CUT TO: A Country Lane near Welton Cross. Day.
MIKE's car halts at the notice board. RUTH is seated alongside MIKE in the front of the car.

CUT TO: In MIKE's Car. Day.
RUTH is looking anxiously at MIKE.

MIKE: Drive on for a couple of hundred yards so
               O'Day doesn't see the car when he leaves.
RUTH: Mike, are you sure you ought to –
MIKE: (*Shaking his head*) He's not going to find the
               boy by asking Lloyd a lot of questions! Don't
               you see, Ruth – one smell of the police and
               he'll be off like a rocket.
MIKE makes to get out of the car. RUTH grasps his sleeve.
RUTH: Be careful, won't you? I don't want anything to
               happen to you now. Not just when we've begun
               to …
*MIKE looks at RUTH. It is a moment of complete tenderness
and understanding between them. He kisses her briefly, then
goes, closing the car door. RUTH is tense and worried as she
starts the car, her eyes watching MIKE set off.*

CUT TO: Longacre Farm. The Living Room.
*O'DAY and CRADDOCK watch LLOYD as he reads the
headlines on a newspaper they have handed to him. He smiles
and hands the paper back to CRADDOCK with a light sigh,
almost of relief.*
LLOYD: Thank the Lord! I thought you were going to
               question me about a stolen car. I'm in the
               secondhand car business, you see, and –
O'DAY: (*Cutting Lloyd short*) I understand, sir. So
               you've no idea how your telephone number
               came to be in Miss Stevenson's address book?
LLOYD shakes his head.
LLOYD: Not a clue.
CRADDOCK: D'you think your wife might have given it to
               her?
LLOYD: My wife and I are separated. She's been living
               in Jersey for the past two years, so she'd hardly
               give anyone this phone number.

CRADDOCK and O'DAY exchange disgruntled glances as LLOYD turns to the drinks table in the window.

CUT TO: Outside Longacre Farm. Day.
LLOYD is at the drinks table, facing the living room window, pouring drinks. MIKE is pressed against the wall alongside the window. He looks carefully around, taking in the geography of the house.

CUT TO: Longacre Farm. The Living Room. Day.
LLOYD: Selby Brooks, did you say?
LLOYD turns to O'DAY and CRADDOCK with the drinks. O'DAY watches LLOYD closely.
O'DAY: That's right, sir. She was a friend of Ruby Stevenson.
LLOYD: I see …
CRADDOCK murmurs "Thanks" as he accepts the drink from LLOYD.
LLOYD: And for some reason or other you assumed I was a friend of both of them?
LLOYD smiles pleasantly and raises his glass. There is something slightly mocking about the gesture. O'DAY is not enamoured with Mr LLOYD.

CUT TO: Longacre Farm. The Kitchen. Day.
The back door latch clicks open, and MIKE enters. He moves quickly to the door leading to the hall and listens. After a moment, he opens this door and moves cautiously into the hall.
CUT TO: Longacre Farm. The Hall. Day.
MIKE tiptoes to the living room door and remains there, listening to the sound of voices.

CUT TO: Longacre Farm. The Living Room. Day.
Lloyd, in cheerful mood, is taking O'DAY's empty glass.

85

LLOYD: I'm sorry I've been such a disappointment to
                you …

*O'DAY gives LLOYD a quick, forced smile and holds out his
hand to CRADDOCK. CRADDOCK passes him the envelope he
has been holding.*

O'DAY: Have you any children, Mr Lloyd?

LLOYD: One. A boy.

*LLOYD looks on, faintly curious, as O'DAY takes the
photograph from the envelope.*

O'DAY: Living with you – or –

LLOYD: He's with my wife. In Jersey.

O'DAY: Is this the boy?

*LLOYD takes the photograph and looks at it. There is not a
flicker of recognition in his eyes.*

LLOYD: If it is – he's changed a lot since I last saw him.

O'DAY: When was that, sir?

LLOYD hands back the photograph.

LLOYD: Just over two years ago. The day my wife left
                me.

O'DAY looks blankly at CRADDOCK.

LLOYD: I must say I'm intrigued by all this, Inspector.
                That you should think this was my son, for
                instance …

CUT TO: Longacre Farm. The Hall. Day.

*MIKE is at the living room door. Suddenly, he moves to the
stairs, climbing swiftly and silently. The living room door opens
as MIKE reaches the landing. O'DAY and CRADDOCK come
out of the living room followed by LLOYD. They cross to the
front door.*

CUT TO: Longacre Farm. The 1st Floor Landing. Day.

There are three rooms on this floor. Two of the doors are open,
the third is closed.

MIKE makes a cursory investigation of the two with open doors, then tiptoes to the third. The floorboard creaks. He stops, holding his breath.
From the hall, we hear the sound of the front door closing.
MIKE puts a hand on the handle of the closed bedroom door.
We hear the sound of O'DAY's car starting outside.
MIKE realises this will cover any noise he might make. He opens the bedroom door.

CUT TO: Longacre Farm. 1st Floor Bedroom. Day.
MIKE looks around the room. There is a single bed with a man's slippers beside it. There are cigarettes and an empty whisky glass on the bedside table. This is obviously LLOYD's own bedroom. MIKE goes quickly to the window peering down.

CUT TO: Outside Longacre Farm. Day.
O'DAY's car is being driven down the drive, away from the house.

CUT TO: Longacre Farm. The Hall. Day.
LLOYD is peering through the hall window watching the car. His amused, cheerful manner has vanished. His brain is racing, seeking a course of action. He makes a decision.

CUT TO: Longacre Farm. 1st Floor Landing. Day.
MIKE comes out of the first floor bedroom as LLOYD starts to ascend the stairs from the hall. MIKE, hearing LLOYD's footsteps, freezes. He goes back into the bedroom.

CUT TO: Longacre Farm. 1st Floor Bedroom. Day.
MIKE flattens himself against the wall behind the door. LLOYD comes to the chest in the room, opens a drawer and tosses shirts and underclothes onto the bed. He is obviously about to make a run for it.

87

MIKE stares at the wardrobe. When Lloyd comes to this, MIKE is bound to be discovered. He braces himself.
LLOYD takes a gun, an automatic, from the drawer in the chest and puts it in his pocket. He picks up a shirt, hesitates, throws it onto the bed and goes out.

CUT TO: Longacre Farm. 1st Floor Landing. Day.
MIKE watches through the opening between the door and the lintel as LLOYD goes into the rear bedroom. MIKE comes out of the first floor bedroom and steps inside the adjacent bedroom. From MIKE's eyeline in the bedroom, we see LLOYD go back into his bedroom carrying two suitcases.

CUT TO: Longacre Farm. The Adjacent Bedroom. Day.
Mike is just inside the room listening intently. He hears suitcase catches being opened; LLOYD's feet moving about on the carpet; a door-catch and the creak of doors opening. MIKE guesses LLOYD is now at the wardrobe. He makes to cross the landing to the stairs to the second floor. He stops. Another sound has engaged the whole of his attention. A curious low rumbling; like a miniature thunderstorm. MIKE looks up at the ceiling, puzzled.

CUT TO: Longacre Farm. 2nd Floor Stairs. Day.
MIKE comes cautiously out of the adjacent bedroom and starts to climb these stairs.

CUT TO: Longacre Farm. 1st Floor Bedroom. Day.
LLOYD is taking suits from the wardrobe. He glances casually upwards as the low rumbling noise starts again, then suddenly stops.

CUT TO: Longacre Farm. 2nd Floor Landing. Day.

MIKE tiptoes towards the closed door at the front of the house. This room is directly over LLOYD's bedroom. He stops at the door, listening. The curious noise has started again. It is obviously coming from inside this room. MIKE carefully turns the handle of the door.

CUT TO: Longacre Farm. 2nd Floor Bedroom. Day.

A BOY kneels on the floor playing with a model electric train (the source of the noise). The BOY adds another truck to the train. When he raises his head again, we see that the boy is PAL, the boy MIKE is searching for.

CUT TO: Longacre Farm. 2nd Floor Landing. Day.

MIKE is now applying pressure to the bedroom door – behind which the boy is playing. The door is locked. MIKE hesitates, wondering what to do next. As he turns, his foot strikes something. He stares down at his feet as the silence is broken by a loud, raucous, clicking noise. The source of the clicking noise is a toy of PAL's, a battery-run miniature tractor. MIKE is momentarily hypnotised by the sound and sight of this noisy monster. Suddenly LLOYD's voice breaks his reverie.

LLOYD's VOICE:(*Off screen*) Pal!

MIKE starts.

CUT TO: Longacre Farm. 1st Floor Landing. Day.

LLOYD is in his bedroom doorway, a jacket over his arm, looking upwards with puzzled irritation.

LLOYD: Pal!

CUT TO: Longacre Farm. 2nd Floor Landing. Day.

MIKE remains motionless as the tractor trundles towards the top of the stairs. There is an unholy clatter as it goes over.

CUT TO: Longacre Farm. 1st Floor Landing. Day.

LLOYD swears under his breath, throws down the jacket, and leaps up the stairs, picking up the toy tractor as he goes.

CUT TO: Longacre Farm. 2nd Floor Landing. Day.

LLOYD moves to PAL's bedroom, taking a key from his pocket. MIKE has vanished.

CUT TO: Longacre Farm. 2nd Floor Bedroom. Day.

PAL stares at the door as the key turns in the lock. The door opens and LLOYD enters irritatedly.

LLOYD: Haven't I told you not to leave your things outside this room? Start packing! We're leaving.

PAL's face lights up. LLOYD moves to the chest and starts taking out PAL's clothes.

PAL: Where are we going?

LLOYD: We're going abroad, and I want you to be ready by …

MIKE has entered the room.

MIKE: I shouldn't bank on that.

LLOYD wheels around to see MIKE standing in the doorway. PAL's eyes light up as he recognises MIKE.

PAL: Dad! It's the man I told you about! The one who got my kite for me …

MIKE addresses PAL, but keeps his eyes riveted on LLOYD.

MIKE: Run downstairs, there's a good chap. I want a word with your father.

PAL looks at his father. LLOYD smiles carefully and nods in assent. PAL looks dubiously from one to the other, then goes out.

LLOYD: You've made one hell of a mistake, my friend, coming here!

MIKE: Why? I knew you'd try and make a run for it …

90

LLOYD takes the automatic from his pocket. MIKE glances at it.

CUT TO: Longacre Farm. 2nd Floor Landing.
Through the partly open door, PAL can see his FATHER with the automatic in his hand facing MIKE.

CUT TO: Longacre Farm. 2nd Floor Bedroom. Day.
LLOYD's face hardens. He is about to shoot.

MIKE: (*Playing for time*) Lloyd, I think there's something you ought to know. Something you've overlooked …

LLOYD: What is it?

MIKE: Why do you think the police came to see you?

LLOYD: (*Surprised by the question*) I know why …

MIKE: (*Shaking his head*) You don't. You may think you do, but …

LLOYD: (*Angry, threateningly*) Well, go on! What is it? Why did they come?

MIKE is slowly, carefully, engineering a toe underneath the model railway.

MIKE: You remember the afternoon – the afternoon you saw Selby?

It is now seen that MIKE and LLOYD are on either side of the railway track.

LLOYD: Go on – get to the point!

MIKE: Well, you made a big mistake that afternoon. Almost as soon as you left the houseboat …

MIKE suddenly jerks up his leg and the railway track lifts into the air. LLOYD starts back. MIKE springs forward, gripping LLOYD's neck. They wrestle, falling backwards against the chest of drawers. A tin on the top of the chest is knocked over. Marbles pour across the floor.

CUT TO: Longacre Farm. 2nd Floor Landing.

PAL watches as MIKE and LLOYD wrestle for possession of the automatic. LLOYD breaks away in the direction of the door, turning to fire at MIKE. PAL gasps involuntarily.

CUT TO: Longacre Farm. 2nd Floor Bedroom. Day.

LLOYD skids on the fallen marbles as he fires. There is the sound of smashing glass as the bullet breaks the window. Simultaneously, MIKE dives at LLOYD as he falls backwards.

CUT TO: MIKE's Car parked near Longacre Farm. Day.

MIKE's car is parked in a country lane.

RUTH, in the driving seat, starts anxiously as she hears the shot and the breaking glass.

CUT TO: Longacre Farm. 2nd Floor Landing. Day.

MIKE and LLOYD hurl through the bedroom doorway to the floor. The automatic skates across the landing to where a nervous, frightened PAL is standing. Terrified, he stares down at the automatic at his feet. MIKE and LLOYD are in a desperate struggle. LLOYD turns violently, catching MIKE on the side of the jaw with his elbow, and scrambles to his feet. MIKE reaches blindly out, catching LLOYD's face. LLOYD crashes to the floor, clawing for the automatic. It is just out of reach. He appeals to PAL.

LLOYD: Give it to me! Give it to me!

PAL remains transfixed. LLOYD wrenches one foot free. The automatic is now just within his reach. He grabs for it. With a sudden decision, PAL kicks the automatic through the banisters. We see it as it falls, falls ... through the stairways to the ground below.

We see LLOYD's enraged face through the banisters as the automatic hits the tiles below with an echoing clatter.

PAL runs into the bedroom, LLOYD following – swearing, cursing. As MIKE moves forward, LLOYD lashes out with maniacal frenzy. There is a cry from PAL.

CUT TO: MIKE's Car parked near Longacre Farm. Day.
RUTH is in the car, waiting anxiously, as before. She starts on seeing something in the direction of the house.

CUT TO: Outside Longacre Farm. Day.
It is obvious now what RUTH has seen. LLOYD is running from the house towards the garage.

CUT TO: Longacre Farm. 2nd Floor Landing. Day.
PAL emerges from the bedroom as MIKE rises unsteadily to his feet. From outside we hear the sound of LLOYD's car starting. MIKE runs downstairs. PAL moves quickly to the banisters. We see him staring down after MIKE – a stricken, pathetic face.

CUT TO: Outside Longacre Farm. Day.
LLOYD's car is roaring down the drive as MIKE runs out of the front door of the house. His angry gesture of defeat is quickly followed by fear and concern.

CUT TO: Inside LLOYD's Car. Day.
The reason for MIKE's fear is seen through LLOYD's windscreen. RUTH is driving MIKE's car towards the gateway – the gap in the fence – hoping to block LLOYD's exit. LLOYD sees the car driven by RUTH. He accelerates savagely.

CUT TO: Outside Longacre Farm. Day.
MIKE is waving wildly to RUTH to stop. She mustn't attempt to block LLOYD's exit.

CUT TO: Inside MIKE's Car. Day.
RUTH is driving determinedly. A flicker of the eyes tells us she has seen MIKE's warning. Stubbornly, she accelerates in an all out attempt to reach the gateway before LLOYD.

CUT TO: The Country Lane. Melton Cross. Day.
Both cars are racing towards the gateway.

CUT TO: Inside LLOYD's Car. Day.
LLOYD's eyes are narrowed, intent on RUTH at the wheel of MIKE's car.

CUT TO: The Country Lane. Melton Cross. Day.
RUTH brakes hard as her car reaches the gateway. LLOYD's car hurtles towards her.

CUT TO: Inside MIKE's Car. Day.
Instinctively, RUTH turns away from what seems an inevitable crash.
There is the scream of brakes; the hissing of skidding tyres. RUTH stares out of the window.
LLOYD: (*Off screen*) Get out of the way!

CUT TO: Inside LLOYD's Car. Day.
LLOYD has stopped within inches of RUTH's car. He rages at her.
LLOYD: D'you hear me? Move that blasted thing out of the way!

CUT TO: Inside MIKE's Car. Day.
RUTH, although weak and shaken, sits immobile.
CUT TO: Inside LLOYD's Car. Day.
Lloyd reaches inside his pocket.

94

CUT TO: Longacre Farm. The Long Grass. Day.

MIKE is cutting through the long grass at full pelt towards the gateway.

CUT TO: Inside MIKE's Car. Day.

RUTH stares into the levelled automatic held by LLOYD. He has obviously recovered this on leaving the house.

LLOYD: Move!

This sounds ominously like the final warning. RUTH's hand moves tremblingly towards the dashboard. LLOYD screams at her insanely.

LLOYD: Move, you bitch! Move!

RUTH snatches the car key from the dashboard and throws herself sideways, clawing for the off-side door handle. LLOYD fires!

CUT TO: Inside LLOYD's Car. Day.

LLOYD tears open the door of his car as he fires shots into MIKE's car.

CUT TO: MIKE's Car. Day.

The offside door is open, but RUTH cannot be seen. One of the bullets may have ... Then we see her scrambling, panic-stricken, to the roadside ditch. She still clutches the car key.

CUT TO: Longacre Farm. The Long Grass. Day.

LLOYD swings around to see MIKE about a hundred yards away. He fires wildly. MIKE drops lows to minimise the target as he continues running towards LLOYD. LLOYD makes a decision and moves to MIKE's car where he swears insanely when he finds the key is not there. He runs back to his own car.

CUT TO: Inside LLOYD's Car. Day.

LLOYD reverses frantically, then turns the car round. Through the windscreen we see MIKE running towards the car. He stops dead in his tracks as LLOYD accelerates.

CUT TO: Longacre Farm. The Long Grass. Day.

MIKE is alarmed as he realises LLOYD's intention.

CUT TO: Inside LLOYD's Car. Day.

All of LLOYD's frustration and fury are now being centred on MIKE now. He is a portrait of sadistic anticipation.

CUT TO: MIKE's Car. Day.

RUTH draws herself weakly up to lean on the bonnet. She raises her eyes to see what's happening. She cries out.

CUT TO: Longacre Farm. The Long Grass. Day.

MIKE is staring at the oncoming car. He looks wildly around. For a fleeting moment his attention is arrested then he starts to run.

CUT TO: Inside LLOYD's Car. Day.

LLOYD's hand is gripped on the wheel. MIKE is running for his life about forty yards ahead. LLOYD's face is now a mask of savage pleasure. The last vestige of veneer has gone. Here is the killer – fully unleashed.

CUT TO: Longacre Farm. The Long Grass. Day.

LLOYD's car is rapidly bearing down on MIKE whose lungs are bursting as he runs and stumbles through the long grass.

A rotten tree branch crunches ominously as the wheels of LLOYD's car speed over it.

MIKE is running towards a long trench, a waterway, probably hoping to leap this to safety. The car is only some twenty yards away when MIKE trips, falling headlong. We hear the roar of the oncoming car.

RUTH has seen MIKE fall and she averts her face with a scream.

There is a loud crash followed by a flutter of frightened birds from the nearby hedges and then complete silence.

RUTH's body sags. She seems about to faint. After a moment, she turns, forcing herself to look. She comes around the bonnet of the car.

RUTH: Mike …

RUTH hurries forward and runs towards LLOYD's car which is still and silent in the distance.

There is no sign of MIKE.

CUT TO: LLOYD's Car in the long grass. Day.

RUTH is approaching from the distance. Breathless, she reaches the car and stares down. The camera tracks back to reveal a felled tree trunk up against the front wheels of the car. This would not have been seen until it was too late. Evidently, MIKE had seen it and banked on the outcome.

RUTH raises her eyes to the unseen LLOYD in the driving seat. She turns quickly away with a shudder.

MIKE: (*Off screen*) Ruth …

RUTH looks up. MIKE is kneeling at the spot where he fell. He rises, his arms groping towards RUTH.

RUTH: Mike! Oh, Mike …

RUTH is striving to control herself, but it has all been too much for her. She is half laughing, half crying as she stumbles into MIKE's arms.

CUT TO: The Drive of Longacre Farm. Day. A little later.

The doors of an ambulance are just being closed. MIKE is talking with CRADDOCK and O'DAY alongside O'DAY's car. They look up as the ambulance driver starts the engine.

97

The ambulance pulls away revealing PAL, standing there, quietly watching the proceedings.

O'DAY, CRADDOCK and MIKE watch the departing ambulance.

O'DAY: There goes the end of one problem …

O'DAY looks across at the lonely figure of the BOY.

O'DAY: And the beginning of another …

CRADDOCK makes no comment. O'DAY turns to MIKE. But MIKE has vanished.

PAL is still watching the ambulance go out of sight. A hand grips his shoulder. He looks up. MIKE is standing there. Any emotion MIKE may feel is successfully hidden. Nevertheless, he cannot bring himself to speak. Not that there is anything needed to be said between them. The BOY gives the barest flicker of a smile – which means a great deal in such circumstances. MIKE indicates that they should go, and he steers PAL gently away.

O'DAY and CRADDOCK watch as MIKE and PAL walk away.

CRADDOCK: … Sometimes problems have a way of cancelling themselves out.

CUT TO: The Country Lane. Melford Cross. Day.

MIKE's car is parked near the gateway of Longacre Farm. MIKE opens the door and PAL gets in alongside RUTH, who is in the back of the car.

CUT TO: Inside MIKE's Car. Day.

MIKE gets in and starts the car.

RUTH: Here! Just a minute, darling!

MIKE turns to see RUTH absorbed in wiping some dirt from PAL's face with a handkerchief. PAL is just as absorbed in RUTH's face. MIKE is ignored completely. He smiles to himself and gently changes gear.

CUT TO: The Country Lane. Melford Cross. Day.

MIKE's car reaches the end of the lane and MIKE is just about to accelerate when suddenly, instinctively, he brakes.

Through the windscreen of the car a cat can be seen leisurely crossing the road. It reaches the other side safely. He glances at RUTH, but she hasn't noticed the cat, she is only interested in PAL. For MIKE it is a moment of memory – instantly forgotten as he drives on.

THE END

From Step in the Dark to Piccadilly zero twelve
The truth behind the script of Step in The Dark
by **Dr. Georg Pagitz**

Based on the correspondence between Francis Durbridge and various people involved, this article reconstructs how a screenplay written by Francis Durbridge called *Step in the Dark* became the German thriller *Piccadilly null Uhr zwölf (Piccadilly zero twelve)*, shot in the autumn of 1963 and premiered on December 31st, 1963.

The present screenplay dates from 1961 and thus from a time when Francis Durbridge was probably the busiest and most successful British crime writer. The success was also due to the fact that the author knew like no other how to serve all media: radio, television, magazines with sequel novels and comics, the book market and later also the theatre industry. Of course, he also worked for the cinema. With the film adaptations of his radio plays and early television serials, he had already gained experience with it from 1946. As we will read here, however, he also wrote other stories specially designed for the cinema.

When his television plays were also produced outside the United Kingdom from the end of the 1950s – with popular actresses and actors from the respective countries – the great international success of Francis Durbridge began. The way for this had already been paved across Europe with the adventures of his radio serial detective Paul Temple. Especially Germany, where there was a real crime thriller fiction hysteria in the 1960s, he was enormously successful – so much so that all media wanted to benefit from him and his name.

After the immense success of *Das Halstuch*, the German version of *The Scarf*, broadcast in January 1962 with Heinz Drache and Albert Lieven in the leading roles, there was no stopping it. TV ratings of 89%, empty streets and the revelation of the main villain before the last episode was broadcast by an aggrieved actor whose film was currently on at the cinema and doing good business except on the night's when the serial was being screened had ensured that Durbridge's first place as the most successful living crime writer had been sealed. The author's popularity took on almost grotesque features, for example, German butchers named a meat dish after him.

Magazines were desperate to publish newspaper serials by Durbridge and theatre producers tried to license Durbridge's play *Murder with Love*, which eventually succeeded when Rowohlt Verlag acquired the rights to it and it became an immense success with various productions. It had a run of 120 performances in Munich, under the title *Wettlauf mit der Uhr* (other plays ran a maximum of 60 to 75 performances), in Hans Schweikart's production of the Ber-lin Hebbel Theater with Albert Lieven, Horst Tappert and Ingrid van Bergen in the title roles it became a gigantic success as *Ein lückenloses Alibi*.

The German cinema had enormous success from 1959 onwards with Rialto Films' adaptations of novels by Edgar Wallace. Other producers struggled to find and produce similarly exciting material. An aspect that had hardly been considered at that point was that the crime fiction fever in Germany had been ignited from 1949 by the regular radio serials with Durbridge's detective Paul Temple and that therefore the ground for this genre had already been paved.

When film producers were searching for new thriller treatments it was only logical and not surprising that they went to Francis Durbridge and wanted to repeat his huge TV successes on the big screen.

Therefore it is not surprising that in early 1962 several producers tried to get hold of some Durbridge material for a cinema production. One of them was Rudolf Travnicek from Munich-based MCS-Film KG. He had no previous experience of making thrillers and had only produced some comedy films such as *Unsere tollen Tanten* (*Our Great Aunts* –1961, with Gunther Philipp and Bill Ramsey) or *Die türkischen Gurken* (*The Turkish Cucumbers* – 1961/62, with Gunther Philipp and Oskar Sima).

Marianne de Barde, who was Durbridge's faithful translator for many decades, represented the British author's interests in Germany together with Harvey Unna who was Durbridge's agent and took care of his radio, television and stage licenses. The translator, who lived on Lake Starnberg, also established the contact with MCS-Film. This is how it came about that the deal was concluded.

They agreed on an option contract for the filming of the screenplay for *Step in the Dark*, translated by Marianne de Barde, which should have been produced in 1962. Durbridge himself notes on the 7th of February that he received an amount of 639 pounds, 15 shillings and 5 pence, the equivalent of about 7,300 Deutschmarks.

In July of the same year, Travnicek decided to exercise this film option. This meant that, according to the contract, several sums of money were due to be paid, 11,000 Deutschmarks immediately, as well as another 11,000 on the first day of shooting and the same sum again on the fifteenth day. In September, Durbridge finally received the finished contract for the film adaptation of *Step in the Dark*. However, filming did not get off the ground. The reason for this was that MCS could not find a film distributor.

In a letter to Francis Durbridge dated June 17th, 1963, the producer explains that he would like to make the film, but that he had not succeeded in getting the major German distribution companies Constantin, Nora and Gloria Film interested in it. He explained about the difficult situation within the German film market, which became more challenging from month to month. Since no other distributor could be found, MCS-Film offered

Step in the Dark to ZDF (the second German tv station) without success, even if this would have been a loss-making business.

In the same letter, MCS asks Durbridge to extend the option to the film by one year, as they had run into financial difficulties due to the production *Flying Clipper* (1962) and could not produce *Step in the Dark* themselves at the moment.

The payments agreed in the contract were still due, MCS asked for a postponement and proposed to Durbridge the option that he could sell *Step in the Dark* to another company, if he could get his money faster by doing that.

Through his agent Harvey Unna, Durbridge replied that he understood the situation, but he added that for various reasons he could not allow a postponement, especially since two other producers had been interested in *Step in the Dark* previously, which had to be rejected at the time due to the commitment of MCS and these producers now did not express further interest in the film adaptation.

The letter of the 26th June 1963 also states that MCS should not have exercised the option if they had not been able to raise the money for the production.

Then there seems to have been some misunderstandings, perhaps due to the fact that Harvey Unna was Durbridge's agent for radio and television, but not for the cinema. In August 1963, Rudolf Travnicek tried to obtain a commitment from him to obtain options on all other Durbridge film material. Unna was probably not so familiar with the procedures in the German film industry and did not reject this idea decisively enough, so that MCS had the impression that they could negotiate with others about the film rights. Furthermore a later document from March 1964 shows that Travnicek's contract for further substance licences intended for Durbridge was never signed.

What exactly happened then cannot be traced exactly from the correspondence between Durbridge, Unna, de Barde and MCS.

Somehow, however, Gloria, one of the big three film distributors finally seemed to be interested in the material (possibly Travnicek had convinced them after all). That's why they wanted to pay the outstanding 11,000 Deutschmarks to Durbridge if he signed a release declaration, which he refused.

The press material for *Piccadilly null Uhr zwölf/Piccadilly zero twelve* claims that

The executive producer Eberhard Meichsner went to London in March 1963 to talk with Durbridge about a feature film. However, since there was a valid contract with MCS and Rudolf Travnicek at that time, this is just as questionable as the thesis contained in Joachim Kramp's book *Hallo! – Hier spricht Edgar Wallace* which tells that Durbridge was invited to Munich to negotiate about a film. For these assertions, as well as for the working title *12 Past 12*, which is often quoted on the internet, there are neither records, notes nor evidence in Durbridge's documents. On the contrary, neither a meeting with Meichsner nor with Gloria is noted in his diary (if such a meeting took place the appointment would probably have taken place with Durbridge's agents). Furthermore there is no trace of income for the film in the author's cash book

In any case, Gloria-Film decided to produce the Durbridge story with their own film company Divina-Film in Berlin. In the end, however, they seemed to lose interest in the original story, probably also because Durbridge had not received the sums originally agreed in the contract with MCS. They apparently thought to be on the safe side it would be better if they invented a completely new story. However, for publicity reasons they did not want to renounce on the use of Durbridge's name and that is why perhaps that four characters names were taken from the original script. These (Mike Hilton, Jack Bellamy, Ruth and Inspector Craddock) were the only thing that was left of Durbridge's original script in the finished film. As we will see below, the author had never seen the final film script and had not been informed about any changes. At the time, Durbridge was busy with far too many other things so he was not able to take a closer look at what was going on. Among other things, he was also working for the renowned producer Dino de Laurentiis on a screenplay called *Zachary*.

Whatever the contractual terms for *Step in the Dark/ Piccadilly null Uhr zwölf*, Gloria Film was already interested in further Durbridge scripts. In November 1963, they negotiated this time through the Curtis Brown agency with Durbridge's film agent Kenneth Cleveland and as a result, the treatments for two Paul Temple adventures were presented to the distributor, as well as treatments for a film called *The Man Who Beat the Panel* and a film called *Deadline for Harry*. In a letter from the Curtis Brown Agency to Durbridge dated November 15th, 1963, it is mentioned that Gloria Film is primarily interested in stories that could be filmed in Germany. On November 28th, Curtis Brown announced that Gloria Film had found great pleasure with the two Temple treatments. They had already approached a successful producer who was very interested in the project: the legendary Artur Brauner with his Berlin based CCC film company, who had experience in the thriller sector through film adaptations by Edgar Wallace and his son Bryan Edgar Wallace or through films such as *Dr. Mabuse* or *Sherlock Holmes*. However, this deal did not come about because Rudolf Travnicek claimed to own the German film rights. Therefore, the planning came to nothing, as can be seen from a later letter dated 29th January 1964. Although both Brauner and Gloria were assured by Durbridge's agency that the rights to the Temple titles would be available, there was never a film adaptation made. The curiosity of this letter is the handwritten addition of Harvey Unna that he wanted to talk to Durbridge personally about Artur Brauner.

Travnicek's assumption of owning the German rights to all Durbridge cinema treatments was due to the misunderstanding described above. In fact, Rudolf Travnicek was back in the game in November 1963 with his MCS-Film KG company and had apparently licensed the rights to *Step in the Dark* to Gloria. Perhaps that's why he was solvent again, because the Curtis Brown agency had offered him the option of a Durbridge treatment called *The Face of Carol West*, which the author had already published in the 1950s as a newspaper serial and in 1962/63 under the title *Sie wussten zuviel* (*They knew too much*) for the German television listings magazine *Bild and Funk* had been rewritten. However, Travnicek did not respond to this offer, according to a later correspondence between Curtis Brown and Durbridge. On 3rd February 1964, the agency finally informed their client, Francis Durbridge, that they informed Mr Travnicek in a letter that he had no option rights on any Durbridge treatments. It wasn't until April 21st that MCS-Film replied: "Please excuse the delay in the matter of the script of *The Face of Carol West* but we had been in discussions with several producers and just got the script back. We do not see any possibility to materialize this project which we think is more suitable for television."

However, Curtis Brown still held back the treatments for *East of Algiers* (German novel title: *Die Brille*, as audio book *Paul Temple und der Foster Fall*) and *Lady in the Villa* (*Die Dame in der Villa*, included in the short story collection *Paul Temple – Die verlorenen Fälle*).

Around the same time (November 23rd, 1963), Divina Film asked Durbridge for an interview for the press release re *Piccadilly null Uhr zwölf* but this didn't happen because Durbridge could say little about the film. In a letter to the film company with current photos of himself and some biographical details, he wrote: "To be frank, I could add very little to the enclosed information. I trust the film is going well and that it will prove a success with both the critics and public."

In truth, however, the author did not seem to have been so convinced of this, because on December 12th, 1963, he wrote a letter to his translator Marianne de Barde asking her if she had seen the final script version of his script. At the same time, he was surprised that the film was now entitled *Piccadilly at Midnight* [sic!]. Durbridge wrote: "The significance of this title escapes me because there was nothing in my script about Piccadilly. I am wondering if the film company have made any drastic changes to the German script." In addition, Durbridge explains in the letter that Divina Film wanted a statement from him for publicity purposes in which they asked him to state that he had written the whole story especially for them and that it was about the London call girl racket in 1963. Durbridge refused, remarking to Marianne de Barde: "I suppose that it's just the usual crazy film world and it's publicity!" Finally, he asks his translator to inform him as soon as she had seen the film.

On December 29th, 1963, two days before the premiere of the film, Marianne de Barde wrote to Francis Durbridge: "I have not seen the final script and I rather shudder at what may have become of your text. However, as you will see from the attached article from the *Münch-ner Abendzeitung*, they seem to have kept your title *Ein Schritt in der Dunkelheit*. I shall keep you posted on that, and up to date with everything else I can find out."

About a month later, on January 26, 1964, Marianne de Barde informed Durbridge's agent Harvey Unna that she had now seen *Piccadilly null Uhr zwölf*. She wrote: "The story shown has nothing whatsoever to do any more with the original script." At the same time, she asks Unna for a copy of the contract to see what rights Divina had to turn the plot into a completely new story.

On January 29th, 1964, Durbridge's film agent wrote to the author that he had learned that *Piccadilly null Uhr zwölf* was doing above average at the box office – except on those evenings when the Durbridge six-part serial, *Tim Frazer – Der Fall Salinger,* was being shown on TV.

On the same day, Hannes, Marianne de Barde's brother, wrote a letter to the agent Harvey Unna. He enclosed the film programme for *Piccadilly null Uhr zwölf* and adds that everyone can see from it that there was nothing left of the original script – except [sic!] two names were given to quite different kinds of character. It also states: "It seems fairly evident that the company has bought solely Durbridge's name and has used no part of what he has written. The whole film script as it stood could be used again, if two names are changed."

Francis Durbridge did not agree to this, even when Marianne de Barde proposed in September 1965 *Step in the Dark* would make an excellent ninety-minute television film for the WDR, as the content was completely unused. Francis Durbridge wrote the word "No" in large letters on this letter on September 30th, 1965, putting an end to the matter. Later correspondence also shows that both Durbridge and Divina Films were uncertain about the legal situation and that Durbridge's refusal to use the material "again" probably came from this. As early as April 1964, Durbridge had a possible lawsuit considered by his lawyer through his agent – in the middle of contract negotiations on other treatments – who wrote: "So far as I can tell from the documents I have, the wording of the granting of rights is so vague that it would be difficult to enforce it but I imagine that Mr Durbridge would be just as embarrassed by a claim from the Germans as by a successful action. Any claim of this kind would be bound to come as far as I can see at a time when I was negotiating other rights and a satisfactory and lucrative deal might then fall through because of the claim."

109

Back to February 1964: At that point, Durbridge had heard a lot about the film, but hadn't seen it. He does not seem to have been very happy about this, because on February 11th he writes a letter to the Westdeutscher Rundfunk (WDR), which had produced most of the German Temple radio serials and nearly all of his television serials. The letter is addressed to Ludwig Schmidt and also to Wilhelm Semmelroth, who was responsible for the production of the so-called street sweepers at that time. Durbridge writes: "There is a film being shown in Germany at the moment, which I am supposed to have written, called *Piccadilly at Midnight.* [sic!] This should be a film version of a script of mine called *Step in the Dark* which Mrs De Barde sold, on my behalf, to a film company about three years ago. I haven't seen the film myself but I understand from Mrs De Barde and her brother that there isn't a single scene left in the film and that the story is completely different from the one I wrote. I thought I would drop you a friendly note about this just in case you, or Herr Semmelroth, or indeed any of your colleagues, see this film and think I have suddenly turned into a genius (if it is very good!) or an idiot (if it is very bad!)."

January 1964 was an intense "Durbridge month" in Germany, because on the one hand the *Piccadilly* film was released, on the other hand the second Tim Frazer serial (called *Tim Frazer - Der Fall Salinger*) was successfully broadcast between 10 and 20 January on ARD. This gave another film producer the idea to benefit from Durbridge's popularity. This time it was a Berlin film producer of Polish descent Sam Waynberg (actually Samuel Wajnberg) and his Planet-Film GmbH company. A letter dated February 11th, 1964, shows that Waynberg was planning to produce a Tim Frazer cinema series. Francis Durbridge agreed to write a 15,000-word treatment with a new Frazer story for £10,000. Waynberg proposed to develop a screenplay from it. In addition, Durbridge would read this screenplay and make his comments

110

about it. If the sum had been paid, Waynberg would have acquired the world rights to the story, with an option for three more Frazer adventures outlined by Durbridge. At the same time, the author agreed not to use them for television adventures. In addition, the agreement stated that there would be no further Frazer serials on tv for a certain period of time in Germany if the contract was concluded (with the exception of agreements already made with the WDR). Furthermore, Waynberg would have the exclusive world rights to Tim Frazer film adaptations for one year.

Ultimately, nothing came of it. What happened exactly is not clear from Durbridge documents, but Durbridge wrote to Curtis Brown on March 21st, 1964, that he had a feeling that the "Tim Frazer" subject was still a "hot" property for Germany and that he was fully prepared to do a deal if the interested party didn't try "any last-minute tricks like Mr Waynberg had".

Apparently, Mr Waynberg had received two letters from Curtis Brown and reviewed them with his lawyers, according to correspondence from April 1964.

A year earlier, Durbridge had told the WDR, that he only wanted to agree to license his third Tim Frazer TV adventure, which had already been shown on the BBC in 1961, if the WDR simultaneously bought the script for *The Desperate People* (*Die Schlüssel*). He insisted on the fact that Tim Frazer III should be produced after *The Desperate People*. Durbridge did not want German audiences to be fixated on this series character and saw the danger of over exposure. In later letters, he even wanted *Melissa* to be produced as the next Durbridge serial after *Tim Frazer – Der Fall Salinger*. Tim Frazer III was eventually dropped by him until 1970, when the WDR insisted against Durbridge's will that Durbridge rewrite the Tim Frazer III script. Therefore the WDR gave him back his scripts for a serial called *Stupid Like a Fox* (later produced by the BBC as *The Passenger*) and *The Circle (*produced as *A Game of*

Murder in the UK, later produced as *Die Kette* in Germany). Durbridge hesitated, but eventually agreed and turned it into *Das Messer* (literally: *The Knife*)– a serial with a similar plot to *Tim Frazer and the Mellin Forrest Mystery* but with different character names and a new villain.

But let's get back to the German-speaking cinema market: among the documents of Francis Durbridge was a treatment called *Tim Frazer and the Melvin Affair*. This could have been the scenario mentioned in the letter to producer Sam Waynberg. In any case, it has nothing to do with the story of the Austrian thriller *Tim Frazer jagt den mysteriösen Mister X (Case 33 Antwerp)*, which started being shown in cinemas on June 12th, 1964.

This was an attempt to jump on the bandwagon of the enormous Tim Frazer television success. However, Durbridge had definitely not licensed any rights to the Melba Film Company in Vienna. When Durbridge learned of the use of his character and name, he was quite upset about it. In the end, however, he granted Melba Film a retroactive license and at the same time prohibited his name from appearing in the opening credits. The alternative would have been to take legal action abroad, which would have cost a lot of money. Therefore, he opted for a pragmatic solution.

Two years later, in May 1966, there were further plans for a Durbridge feature film. *Hörzu* (19/1966) reported that Durbridge was writing a feature film called *Scotland Yard Calls Paul Temple*, which was based on the 1948 film *Calling Paul Temple* (German: *Wer ist Rex?*) which was based on the radio serial *Send for Paul Temple Again!* from 1945. In the issue dated 27/1966 the magazine had to publish a letter from Francis Durbridge, who wrote in it: "I would like to state: All rights to the Paul Temple stories lie with me. I didn't allow any film company to make a film of it." The unnamed Munich film production company countered in the same issue that the planned project was the remake of a thriller shot in 1946, but that shooting could only begin once the legal situation had been clarified. Nothing more was heard of this project. Durbridge's correspondence also contains a letter from the *Hörzu* editor-in-chief, who apologizes to the author for the false report. They had been "misinformed".

Finally, it should be mentioned that another well-known German film producer, Gyula Trebitsch, came into play in 1968 to produce two Durbridge treatments, but for television: After the WDR had rejected the scripts for *Bat Out of Hell* (later version: *Wie ein Blitz*) and *The Circle* (the former English version being *A Game of Murder,* (later German version: *Die Kette*) and decided in 1967 that they would no longer produce any more Durbridges after *Ein Mann namens Harry Brent (A Man Called Harry Brent)*, Trebitsch tried to use his contacts to the ZDF to film them for this station. Apparently, this did not come about, because the WDR finally decided that the Durbridge brand could not be let go to the competition.

Finally, let's come back to *Step in the Dark*. After Francis Durbridge had decided not to have this material filmed anymore – neither for cinema nor for television – he made a novel of it. In May 1969, Hodder & Stoughton released *The Pig-Tail Murder*. This thriller tells the story of *Step in the Dark*. In Germany, the novel was published as *Im Schatten von Soho* in the same year by Goldmann-Verlag as *Taschenkrimi Nr. 3218*. The story also was published in a Slovenian edition (*Papirnati zmaj)* (literally: *The Paper Dragon*)), a Dutch (*De haarvlecht* (literally: *The Braid*)), a Polish (*Warkocz śmierci* (literally: *Braid of Death*)), an Italian (*Mezz'ora per vivere, mezz'ora per morire* (literally: *Half an hour to live, half an hour to die*)) and a French translation (*L'enfant au cerf-volant* (literally: *The Child with the Dragon*).

The title *Step In the Dark* is to be understood metaphorically and does not refer to any particular scene in the plot.

Finally, my special thanks go to Nicholas Durbridge, who provided me with many pages of original correspondence from his father for the reconstruction of the events surrounding *Step in the Dar*k.

Printed in Great Britain
by Amazon